A Rebel in Jericho

The Jericho Resistance: Book One

Mimi Milan

Cover by Kirk DouPonce
DogEared Design
www.dogeareddesign.com

Published by Eaton House
P.O. Box 19795
Charlotte, NC 28219-0795

ISBN – 978-0-9964353-0-7

For speaking engagements, interviews, or other
inquiries, please contact the author at:

www.writemimimilan@gmail.com
www.mimimilan.com
www.facebook.com/AuthorMimiMilan

Printed and bound in the United States of America.

Join the resistance!

The Jericho Resistance Series

A Rebel in Jericho

You just made a difference!

Thank you for choosing this novel. Twenty percent of all proceeds goes to the fight against human trafficking.

What readers are saying about A Rebel in Jericho:

"I thought it was very intriguing, filled with a lot of suspense. It's the kind of book I can see as a movie."

E. Lodato

"A delightful blend of drama, romance and self-discovery."

Tiffany C.

"Romance, intrigue and danger! It's an exciting adventure as the reader joins Catalina on her perilous journey through the underbelly of Mexico's dark side."

P.H.

To my family.

Thank you for humoring me every time I said,
"Listen to this one."

Then you all did something amazing...
and told me the stories were good.

Did you know…?

- Slavery still exists today in the form of human trafficking.
- Human trafficking: (noun) The ILLEGAL movement of people – usually to be used in forced labor, sexual exploitation or organ harvesting.
- Nearly THIRTY MILLION individuals are enslaved right now.[1]
- Of the possibly 800,000 humans trafficked every year, 80% are female and HALF are children.
- The United States in one of the top three places for trafficked humans.
- The average cost of a slave is $90, and the industry generates approximately $32 BILLION annually.
- Sex trafficking plays a HUGE role in the spread of HIV and other STDs. By fighting human trafficking, we are fighting the spread of diseases in our society!
- The Bible proves that God finds the abduction of another as an abomination; such an act was punishable by death. (Ex. 21:16)
- By purchasing this book, you are helping in the fight against human trafficking. Thank you so much for taking a stand in what is right. As a friend of mine often says, May you be "blessed and highly favored" today and always.

---

[1] All facts can be verified via a simple internet search.

Acknowledgments

There are so many individuals who contributed to the creation of this book. I apologize if I leave anyone out. Rest assured, the services you provided were priceless. This book would not exist without your help.

To God, the Master Creator and Original Storyteller, goes all thanks for giving me the gift of stories. Each and every single one of them comes from You, and I pray that my writing has done justice to them.

Thank you, Caryl McAdoo, for being more than an amazing writer. The wealth of information you shared with me is beyond compare. It would have taken a whole library to learn what you've taught me! You are a never-ending source of encouragement, and I consider myself "blessed and highly favored" to know you.

Kirk DouPonce, I can't praise your work enough. There is a reason you're one of the best in the industry. Your book covers are true to the stories they represent. Thank you for bringing mine to life! I look forward to seeing what you've got in mind for the rest of my books.

Dora Hiers, writer extraordinaire, you are a wonderful critique partner. Thank you for praising my strengths, and pointing out my weaknesses. My writing is all the better for it.

Emily Lodato, Patricia Highton, Tiffany Claudio, Lenda Selph, and Karen Schwee… *YOU LADIES ROCK!* Thank you so much for being awesome beta readers. Your input was invaluable. I hope you enjoy book two as much as this one.

To my husband, Memo, thank you for so many things. Above all, for introducing me to a world outside that which I always knew. Despite the hardships we endured and the terrors that we suffered, your country is beautiful. I hope to see it again one day.

Finally, I give thanks to the woman who instilled in me a love for books (and nature). Thank you, Aunt Yvonne, for buying me that book about horses. This one's for you.

"He is rescuing and delivering and performing signs and wonders in the heavens and on the earth…"

-   Daniel 6:27

Chapter One

Charlotte, North Carolina – June 1918

"Now folks, we only have a few more pails left."

Catalina Santé's dark eyes glistened with excitement. The Reverend's claim that seven lunch boxes were already sold sent a delicious shiver down her spine. Only a few more to go before hers finally came up for auction. She silently ticked off the ones that were left on her lace covered fingers. The feel of the embroidered fabric growing damp from her sweaty palms summoned the irritating reminder of the stifling heat. Of course, she could blame no one other than herself for her discomfort. The excitement of the day's events had thoroughly jumbled her mind, and she forgot all about the usefulness of things like hand fans and parasols. Now the relentless summer sun beamed down on the small church yard, making all the attendants completely miserable. Catalina would've surrendered her finest dress for a cool breeze or a refreshing drizzle.

Thunderstorms… Snow!

Really, anything would be a welcomed change from the stifling heat that plagued the town.

Tugging at her collar, she turned her focus back to the auction block and assessed the proceedings, determination stiffening her spine. With less than fifteen minutes into the bidding, this event had proven to be the most successful one the church hosted thus far. Of course, speculation proved easy as to the reason for such achievement. Either the young men of the congregation had mothers that refused to feed the lot, or a few sweethearts had been informed to bid on specific boxes. However, none of them could be faulted for doing so. The war had stripped the town of so many good men, leaving everyone grateful for those that remained...

Or returned almost healthy and whole.

Catalina lifted one gloved hand and waved it around, fanning herself as best she could. Why were the bidders taking so long to respond? It seemed as though they were each waiting for the dramatic announcement of "last call." She didn't want to deny them their fun, but still. The sooner they got to her box, the quicker everyone could find some shade. She craned her neck around, searching out the girls in the crowd who still had lunch pails left. Then Reverend Livingstone's next announcement brought her attention back to the podium.

"I'd like to remind the congregation that Christ told us to give freely." He announced. "In doing so, we'll all be receiving a beautiful organ for the church. So how much do I hear for this handsome box laced in mint green velvet? It's filled with mouth-watering vittles of country fried steak, green beans and biscuits with gravy." The Reverend made a show of smelling the contents. "Ah, yes. Certainly the way to any man's heart!"

"Two bits," little Billy O'Neal hollered out as he held up a couple of shiny coins. A light chuckle rose from the crowd and even Catalina guessed that he bet on his sister's box. Tiffany's face burned a fiery red as bright as her hair.

Catalina shook her head, feeling sorry for her and counted the blessing that her own brother, Gabe, currently attended medical school. He may have been studying to be a doctor, but everyone knew he had a wicked sense of humor. If he had been in attendance, then he would have pulled the same stunt as the O'Neal boy.

"A dollar," a huskier voice interrupted her thoughts. Everyone turned to acknowledge Peter Price as the bidder. A few of the wealthier families often referred to him as little more than a poor sharecropper. However, nothing could have been further from the truth. The investment in a few acres and some backbreaking work proved valuable, and quickly made him the owner of an enormous spread. His land grew every fruit and vegetable agreeable to it, standing in awe or envy of anyone who saw his prized Scuppernongs.

Generous, courteous... Catalina smiled. Things were turning out well for her childhood friend.

"Five dollars," Mr. O'Neal spoke up. A pointed look in Peter's direction silently informed the young man that it would cost him to eat lunch with Tiffany O'Neal.

Peter grinned at the challenge, mischief flashing across his face.

"I'll put down a ten spot and much more," he countered. "We're talking about the blessing of a fine, sturdy home and a secure future with any luxury I can afford."

A few gasps – one of them from Catalina – arose from the onlookers as all clearly heard Peter state his intentions. Looking as pleased as any father could be, Mr. O'Neal conceded to the confident declaration.

"I suppose you have something to discuss with me at dinner tonight. Am I right, son?"

"Yes, sir."

A murmur rose from the crowd and Mrs. O'Neal could be heard mumbling about needing to make preparations. Catalina stifled a giggle as she watched the woman hastily pull her round form from her seat and stumble through the group. She beamed at the idea that the evening would end with Peter asking for Tiffany's hand in marriage.

"Well, that leaves us with only two boxes." Reverend Livingston tried to redirect the attention back to the bidding as Peter Price claimed his box. He placed Tiffany's hand in the crook of his arm, staring down at her with adoration. Little Billy toted a second box and trailed close behind, acting as chaperone.

What would it be like to be whisked off by her beloved to enjoy a private lunch filled with tender moments and quiet laughter? Catalina sighed at the romantic notion of it all, missing every word of the bidding going on.

"Ouch," she cried out as her mother's elbow dug into her side. The Reverend had begun the bid on the last box – her lunch pail.

"We've got some of the finest fried chicken in here, folks. I think I might smell some mashed taters, collard greens and—" Reverend Livingston paused dramatically. "What is that?" He made yet another demonstration of sniffing the outside of the box. "Oh, that's got to be a mighty delicious slice of apple pie. What will we start the bidding at?"

"One whole dollar," Catalina's father waved a single bill in the air. She glared at her father. He feigned a look of innocence. "What? I happen to be hungry."

"And you can eat at home," interjected his wife. She elbowed him back into place. "Leave the bidding to the younger folks and stop tormenting your daughter."

Gian Carlos had the decency to look remorseful, contrition painting his face as his wife reprimanded him. Everyone laughed, and he nodded to the Reverend to continue the bidding.

"One and fifty."

"Two."

Catalina heard the Johnson brothers vie for her box much the same way they competed for her attention when they were in grade school. It had been cute then, but it most certainly wasn't now. When were they ever going to learn that she had no interest in settling down?

Well, that wasn't entirely true. She did indeed desire to marry. That key point had won the argument when her father initially refused to send her to college. Her mother had championed for her by suggesting the usefulness of an educated wife.

"But, Amor." Her father had argued. "Look at how well you've done. You had even less of an education, and you're the most successful seamstress in all of Charlotte. A few more orders like the ones you've recently received would cover the expenses to have a shop of your own."

"That is true." Mrs. Santé had countered, "But what if sewing was the only skill your daughter learned, and then our business went under one day? She would have to go work for someone else. Is that what you want, Carlos? Your daughter risking her life like those poor girls at The Triangle Shirtwaist Factory?"

Even though it had occurred in Manhattan, the news traveled jack rabbit quick all over the country. The employers of the renowned clothing company had refused the workers well-deserved breaks, barring escape doors and locking their employees in. There was no escape for the women when an accidental fire claimed the building.

The last match in the powder barrel, it blew apart any rebuttal Mr. Santé could conceive. He finally broke down and gave his word that she could go.

The memory of that triumphant day started to fade as Catalina sat at attention and shifted her focus back to the bidding. She let out a disappointed sigh when she heard the Johnson brothers still warring over her lunch pail, outbidding each other by mere pennies.

"Two and fifty cent," Wayne Johnson called out.

"Two and fifty-five." His brother, Will, crowed back.

Catalina shook her head. Why didn't they seem to understand that she held no interest in becoming a farmer's wife? Any woman who married into the Johnson clan was guaranteed a life consumed with slopping out a pig pen.

Well, that was the last thing Catalina planned on doing. She was a woman designed for upscale city living. If she could obtain something as difficult as a college degree, then she could certainly manage a household with a prestigious name.

And "Johnson" was not it!

"Mama," Catalina hissed between her clenched teeth as the bidding continued amongst the farm boys. "Surely there is something you can do. Encourage Papa to speak up. Anything but this!"

Her mother gave her head a firm shake and dismay set in.

Catalina buried her nervous hands within the folds of her dress. Where was Ben? He had promised he would attend the social and bid on her lunch. If he or someone else didn't speak up soon, then she would end up spending the rest of the afternoon with either Wayne or Will Johnson. A horrid vision streaked across her mind and she saw herself standing at the altar with each brother on either side of her, fighting over who would get to say "I do."

Cat shuddered at the idea. Surely there was someone – anyone – willing to send these boys back to the farm!

She glanced around to see if any salvation was at hand, and met the dour stare of a peculiar deputy. His hair was so dark that it almost looked blue, and the same held true for his eyes. They reminded her of the sea after a storm had settled on the Carolina coast. Catalina watched him for only a moment longer before remembering that she had seen him in her mother's dress shop once. He certainly seemed pleasant enough. Still, she hoped he hadn't been the person bidding on her pail. He probably lived in some rundown shack.

"Well, that leaves us at six dollars," declared Reverend Livingston. "Do we have a higher bidder, or is this delectable lunch going to the fine young man down front?"

The Johnson brothers glared at each other. Which of them had gotten the last bid in?

"Alright, then. If I don't hear a call for six and fifty for this fine meal… Going once, going twice—"

"Seven dollars."

Catalina's head jerked up and a few dark curls fell from her pinned hair. Balancing on the tips of her leather shoes, she scanned the crowd, eager to thank the bidder for saving her from a date with the Johnson boys. Where was he? She wiped her wet palms down the sides of her dress, worried over who she would end up eating lunch with after all. Studying the possible suitors, her breath caught when she spied the dark deputy again. His eyes locked with hers, the corners of his mouth slowly curving into a dimpled grin. He gave her a bold wink as the Reverend again announced a last call.

Was he the bidder?

Catalina thought on the idea of spending the afternoon with a handsome deputy. Remembering the Johnson brothers, she decided that there were certainly worse ways to spend the afternoon. She smiled back as the Reverend raised the gavel in the air.

"Ten dollars."

Everyone's head turned to make out the speaker, Catalina simply sighed with relief. She did know the sound of that cultured voice. It was the same one that whispered hurried endearments behind the stacks of flour in her father's bodega. She didn't even need to look up to certify that Benjamin Monroe had easily outbid all the other gentlemen in the group.

Maybe he'll make a declaration of his intentions, like Peter and Tiffany. She inwardly hoped the next announcement her father placed in *The Charlotte Observer* would feature her engagement to Ben Monroe, instead of the bags of sugar they had on sale.

"Any takers on ten dollars?" the Reverend asked. No one seemed inclined to bid. No matter how delicious the fried chicken was, betting higher on such fare made a man look ridiculous. That kind of money was a whole week's worth of groceries for simple folks like the Johnson brothers.

Sure enough, they lost interest and fell out of the bidding.

The Reverend slammed down his wooden gavel.

"The last boxed lunch is sold to Brother Monroe! Will the lass who prepared this step forward, please?"

Catalina graciously bowed her head as she stood to claim her spot next to the lunch pail, the matching silk making it look as if she were simply holding a large, pea-green purse. Ben walked to the front of the crowd, his confident stride reassuring Catalina that all would be well. He offered his arm to her and she latched on, a lively mixture of excitement and relief caused her stomach to flutter.

"I was thinking it would be nice to take a ride today. I brought the wagon instead of the car." Ben dipped low and whispered, the heat of his breath tickling her ear. Warmth spread through her neck and cheeks. She casually threw back a glance at her parents. They were already surrounded by a group of their peers, undoubtedly congratulating them on such a good match. "So what do you think?"

"Oh, well. I don't know." Catalina snapped her attention back to Ben. The bright sun made his blond mane shine, causing his hazel eyes to appear even more intense than usual. They beseeched hers, the gold in them bright with expectancy. She wavered momentarily, knowing that her reputation could be ruined if the two of them were caught alone. Even if they were on their very best behavior, people would speculate about more than a simple luncheon. Not that she would have caved to temptation, of course. No matter how handsome she thought Ben to be, she wouldn't allow anyone in town thinking she was available to just any man. Catalina turned her doe eyes to Ben and offered a half-hearted excuse. "My mother just made me this dress. I'd hate to ruin it."

Quick on the take, Ben chuckled. "That's never stopped you before."

Catalina bit her lip, hesitant to admit that he was right. She had ridden her own horse while wearing a dress plenty of times, even doing so in her Sunday best. She tried another approach. "I suppose that may be true, but it still doesn't change the fact that this heavy outfit will make it rather difficult to get on the horse." She shrugged a sly smile as though they had run out of options.

"Don't worry about that." Ben ran a frustrated hand through his hair. "I can help you up, as well as dismount – the same as any true gentleman would."

Catalina frowned at his patronizing tone. He quickly smoothed over any little doubt. Then he leaned in close to her, his low voice causing her breath to catch as he spoke.

"Besides, there's something I wish to speak to you about, darling."

He looked at her with such intensity that it made her feel lightheaded. A giddy sensation bubbled up inside, forcing Catalina to nod in agreement. She stared into his incredible eyes. They were filled with never-ending promises about what the future held for the two of them. Spending a few short hours alone surely wouldn't cause any damage. Besides, wasn't it obvious? Benjamin Monroe planned on asking for her hand in marriage! It wouldn't matter much what anyone thought of them after she said those magical words "I do."

"Very well," she consented and followed him to the wagon. She watched as he unhitched the horses, handing her the reigns so he could unload a couple of riding blankets and saddles from the wagon. A few minutes later, she was sitting astride a chestnut mare. She allowed Ben to guide her towards Sugar Creek as she chanced a peek behind her, and caught the intense stare of the deputy.

Ignoring the frustrated look on his face, she faced forward again… wondering why she felt disappointed that they wouldn't be lunching together.

Chapter Two

Ben tied his horse up to a tree and made his way back to Catalina. He stared up at her with a playful air.

"Hmmm. You seem to ride fine in a dress. Maybe you should give me a demonstration as to how a lady dismounts in one."

Catalina gasped. "Ben! You wicked thing."

Ben laughed as he reached up and placed his hands on her waist. He helped her off the horse and unceremoniously placed her on the ground.

"There you go. Just as I promised."

Now that wasn't romantic at all. Catalina dipped her head to hide her disappointment.

"Thank you." She forced a happy guise and reached for the green pail. She held up their lunch like a grand prize. "So do you want to find out what ten dollars tastes like?"

"Indeed." Ben said as he got out the blanket, wasting no time to prepare a spot on a nearby knoll. Catalina sat down on the mound and pulled out the cooled fried chicken. They ate to the bubbling sounds of the creek washing over them, the sun sitting on the water like a large gold disc.

"I have a confession to make." Catalina began stuffing the remaining lunch in her pail. "The only hand I put towards this meal were the chocolates." She scrunched her slender nose at him, wondering what he thought of her inability to cook.

Ben waved away her admission. "Why would you have prepared the lunch? That's what servants are for."

His cool tone splashed over her, raising the hair on the back of her neck. An unexpected silence settled over them. Why did his words bother her?

She busied herself again, wiping away at invisible crumbs when Ben stood and picked up a small rock from the ground. He threw it as far as he could before stuffing his hands into his pocket. The rock created ripples that grew outward; a slight breeze encouraged the small waves to swell.

Ben continued to stare at the water as he began a diatribe of what he believed made a good marriage.

"You know, managing a household is much like managing a business." His voice grew serious. "The mistress of the house needs to understand household finances and how to best utilize them. She ought to realize the tasks that need to be completed and how to best delegate the workload to the hired help. That way everything is done in a timely manner." Ben began pacing as he listed the duties of a wife, ticking each one off the tips of his fingers. He paused momentarily and Catalina thought she could finally respond. But he began again. "As if that's not enough, she must be able to stop everything on a moment's notice to entertain any guests who happen by. All the while she has to remain a poised and sophisticated example for her peers and children. And those are just her duties to the home! There are still wifely and motherly obligations to be covered, as well. I can only imagine it is quite an exhausting position."

Ben finally stopped and let out a loud sigh.

Poor man, Catalina thought. *Is he really so worried that I'll turn him down?*

She chewed on her bottom lip, curious to witness this side of Ben. He always seemed so sure of everything. She wondered about another possibility – that maybe he was questioning her capacity to meet the demands of marriage. Oh, how she wanted to reassure him! Her professors had taught her much more than literature and mathematics. Countless days had been spent learning what her place in the home would entail. She could run a household as well as her father could run his business! And the idea of being a wife and mother? She was more than up to the task...

So long as she was marrying a Monroe.

Catalina cleared her throat in an attempt to gain Ben's attention.

He glanced up and rewarded her with a tight smile.

"Those are the traits I hope I will find in my wife," Ben snapped his head up, a compassionate smile painting his face as he approached again. He sat down across from her, the empty lunch basket offering the only wall between them. His hand rested on it and his tone grew soft. "That's why I asked you here today." His gaze bore into her.

Cat could feel herself being swept away on all sorts of emotions. Elation seized her body with the notion that the time had finally come to say "yes," so she allowed herself a flirtatious moment.

"Why, Ben. I never realized you thought so highly of me. Allow me to return the compliment by saying that I think the way you handle your father's business is a sheer stroke of genius. And the dedication to travel three counties as you have done for the past year? Well, that's the mark of greatness." She placed her hand upon his and flashed a coy, little smile.

"Yes, well… Those are only my duties until my brother, Christopher, returns home from the war," Ben gave a disdainful sniff as he removed her hand and let it drop to her side. "But back to the issue at hand… I know we've spent quite a bit of time together in the last couple of months. In fact, I'm sure half the city is speculating that we're betrothed to one another."

Oh, come on already and ask me. I'm going to say yes, silly man!

"So, that's why I wanted you to be the first to know that I've already entered an agreement with Mr. Harrington to marry his eldest," he continued on as though embarrassed at the thought. "I'm sure you're acquainted with the girl. Her name is Mary. She participates in the ladies quilting circle with you and your mother."

A loss of words produced a guttural sound. Catalina stared, dumbfounded. The words washed over her like cold water and a sickening feeling settled in the pit of her stomach. She felt as though she had fallen off a horse; the wind being knocked out of her and offering no sign of relief as heat ebbed through her chest. For a moment, she was so paralyzed with anger that she could do little more than stare at Ben, her mouth gaping open, eyes wide with shock. When the small white dots begin to collect in her vision, and her fiery lungs pleaded for a reprieve, she finally sucked in. The hot summer air did little to relieve the pain in her chest.

"What's the meaning of this?" Catalina jumped up from her spot on the blanket, all the rage and indignity a woman could possess evident as her hands planted firmly on her hips. She glowered down at him. "Why would you enter such a foolish arrangement? Like you said – half the city thinks we're going to marry. Even my mother was speaking of it just this morning! And why should she think any different? You've spent the past few years practically chasing me down!" Catalina threw her hands up in the air and began pacing. Then she spun back on her heel, pointing an accusing finger as she fumed again. "I remember when I couldn't step into my father's store for even two minutes before you would come rushing in to whisper sweet endearments. And you may have thought no one was listening, but you would be mistaken, Sir. My father was hanging onto every little word! Oh, yes, and they were pretty little words indeed. They persuaded me to give you privileges meant only for my intended – holding my hand and walking me home." Lowering her voice only succeeded in fueling the rage Catalina felt inside, and she hissed. "Why, you've spoken to me as intimately as a lover. And now you're telling me you're marrying a Harrington!"

Thunder cracked overhead, startling both of them. A cool breeze pricked her skin. She shivered, her resolve beginning to waiver. Catalina let out a wretched sob.

"Please don't cry, kitten." Calling her by the pet name he had bestowed on her, Ben reached out. The back of his hand trailed down the side of her face, tender and questioning.

She wasn't one to be taken in, though. Not anymore!

Jerking away from his touch, Catalina raced toward the tall oak where the horses were leashed and wrapped her arms around the tree. Its rough bark dug into her soft skin, encouraging her to unleash a stream of salty tears. She cried, her chest heaving as if air had suddenly become a precious commodity.

"I do care for you, Cat." Ben came up beside her. "You're honest and loyal… and no man in town would deny your beauty. If things were different, I'd marry you right here and now."

Frustrated, Catalina threw her hands up in the air before bringing them down and planting them firmly on her hips. "Then how could you choose to marry someone else?" Her voice, raw and throaty, sounded as a low growl when she demanded an explanation.

Ben looked up at the sky, watching the sun disappear behind graying clouds. The sudden change in weather seemed appropriate for what he had to say. "I suppose I can tell you the truth – not that I owe you anything."

Not that he owed her anything? Of all the— Catalina stifled a retort that hung on the tip of her tongue.

Ben turned away from her accusing eyes and began to pace. Time stretched out before her as she waited a long minute for him to continue.

"I know we had spoken a bit before you left town, and I felt like there was some promise in our newfound friendship." He paused and looked back towards Cat before continuing. "But the time that you were away at school proved quite difficult for me. After all, I am a man and men have needs. So, while I was doing business in other towns, I frequented a few places where I could have those needs… eh… *serviced*."

Catalina stared at Ben, trying to comprehend what he was saying. Was she hearing him correctly? He had said "places." It sounded as though he was confessing to behaving indecently with – not just one – but several other women. She processed his heavy words. The weight of them made her jaw drop.

"Yes. You guessed it," he confirmed her assumption. That's when she recognized something more than the absence of guilt. The eye roll; a haughty air of entitlement. The behavior fit his confession. "I could have gone on living without ever telling a soul, too. I had every intention of marrying you – hadn't thought there would be anything standing in my way, though. I even stopped wasting my time on wayward trash as soon as I heard of your return." He had walked back towards her, stopping beneath a low-hanging branch. Irritated, he picked some of the leaves off and threw them into a sudden gust of wind. He sniffed as though something offensive had offended him. "Unfortunately, I wasn't as careful as I should have been. I was approached last week while on business in Gastonia. It would seem as if one of the little tramps got pregnant, and declares I'm the father! As if there couldn't be a dozen other possibilities. Now she expects me to help provide for the illegitimate creature once it's born."

Snorting at what seemed like a ridiculous idea, Benjamin had spat out the last bit of information as though completely disgusted.

Catalina couldn't believe what she was hearing. And she didn't know which angered her more – his horrible hidden secret or his snooty attitude.

Did he think he was the victim? Or that he had no hand in the matter? That it was solely the woman's fault for being with child?

And he planned to cover it all up!

Fury simmered to a boil, and her clenched hands turned into white knuckled fists.

"What it all comes down to," Ben rolled on, "is that Robert Harrington found out through his own dealings in the town."

"Robert Harrington?" Catalina steamed with exasperation. "Why in the name of Jehoshaphat would one of the largest cotton farmers in all of North Carolina be interested in *your* wayward behavior, like he doesn't have enough to manage? We are still talking about the same Harrington. Right? Owner of Catawba Mills?"

"The same." Ben grimaced when her anger washed over him, hanging his head much like a sad puppy. "He approached me yesterday with a proposition I couldn't refuse. Marry one of his daughters, or become public ridicule when he informs everyone in town the particulars of my ruination."

His forlorn look used to weaken her knees. Not anymore! Catalina remained unmoved, fury steeling her spine. He played her with such ease. How many others? Pity the woman who carried his child! She squared off to face him, fists on her hips. "Why would he care to blackmail you like that? No father would want his daughter to marry a man without any scruples." She jabbed a finger in his chest. "A man like you!"

Ben backed up, ignoring the heated clip of each word. "He would if it meant saving his family from destitution." His glare turned intense. "Remember that crazy storm we had a while back?"

"You mean two years ago? The July storm that flooded the mercantile and sew shop?"

He nodded.

She had been summoned from the new campus dormitory for an emergency call in the wee hours of the morning. The operator on the other end had patched her brother, Gabriel, through, who informed her that the family wouldn't be able to make their planned visit that weekend. All because of twenty-two inches of rain that had destroyed nearly everything. Both the mercantile and sew shop had been flooded from the twenty-two inches of rain. It had taken the better part of a week to restore both their home and business. "I remember it. What does that have to do with Robert Harrington, though?"

"Well, Harrington had just sunk a ton of money into building a factory along the Catawba River. Then he filled it with his latest harvest." Ben paused for a moment as the weight of what he was saying slowly sunk in. "He lost fifty-nine bales of cotton! They had washed away, along with half the foundation and the main bridge to Gastonia."

"Then he lost everything." Catalina shook her head, empathy battling with anger. One of the wealthiest families in the entire county had been reduced to nothing with a single, violent act of nature.

"So I could marry one of his daughters and increase both our holdings," Ben continued, "or decline and risk losing everything once he informed my father – and probably everyone else in town – what had come to pass. Now do you understand, Cat? Why I couldn't let my family name be blackened like that? I had no choice but to agree to his demand, and chose the more tolerable of the two girls."

"Yet, you thought it completely acceptable to pursue a match with me while sharing yourself with some saloon tramp?"

Ben pulled on his vest, his chin lifting at a haughty angle. "I already explained to you that I was faithful from the moment I heard of your return."

"Oh, like that small effort accounts for all the hotfooting while I was gone! And what about that woman and her poor babe? Or of Mary Harrington for that matter? She'll be completely mortified when she learns that she's marrying a complete scoundrel."

"Now that's where you're wrong, kitten." Ben reached out and grabbed Catalina by the arms. His voice held a menacing threat as he shook her, his fingers digging into her delicate skin. "You're not going to breathe a word of this to anyone, or I'll leave your name so tattered that no man will ever want anything to do with you – not even those pitiful Johnson boys! You keep your mouth shut about everything I've told you. In return, I'll allow you to tell everyone that it was *you* who refused me. You can tell them any lie you want. Say that you didn't want to live in high society, fell in love with some country bumpkin or anything else your little mind can conjure up."

"But, but…"

His hands tightened, squeezing the flow of blood through her arms, and they grew sore under Ben's firm grip. Scanning her surroundings, she was suddenly aware of how dangerous the situation could become.

Utterly alone in a forest, evening settling in. The earlier glint of sunshine on the water was fading fast. They were secluded. No one would hear her cries for help. Any scream would be swallowed up like a rock in a pond.

"What about the woman?" Catalina tried reasoning with him. "Surely she'll come looking for you to make good on what you've done. Then everyone will know the truth anyway."

An evil gleam shimmered in Ben's eyes, something hard and downright frightening marring his smooth features. How could she have ever considered him attractive?

"No one's gonna' know anything." He spoke, slow and careful. "Robert Harrington would never let some little floozy hurt one of his daughters. He's already told me that after the wedding, he'll have a few of his boys take care of any remaining issues. Now all that's left is to make sure you're not gonna' squawk. Keep some sense in that pretty little head of yours, and maybe we can reach some sort of… *agreement*… after I say my vows."

He relinquished one of her arms to run a finger down the side of her face. Catalina shook, disgust threatening to spill from her throat. How could he possibly think that she was one of those kinds of girls?

"I would never! I am a good, upstanding woman with values, Benjamin Monroe." She pounded on his chest with her one good arm, and he loosened his hold on the other a little. "I thought you had some, too!"

"Oh, please. Don't start that tripe with me." He ignored her cry of indignation. "What? Do you think you're some good little Christian just because you go to church on Sundays? Is that it?"

"No," Catalina declared. She mostly went to church because her parents expected it of her. Still, the fact that she hadn't attended regularly while away at school didn't mean that she had completely lost her faith. She still believed God was real.

Benjamin interrupted her thoughts.

"I didn't think so. Church is for making the right social connections and meeting business associates. Look at any partnership in this town – business or marriage – and you'll see as much. So, don't try playing that holier-than-thou card with me. You're no different than any other money grubber."

"Well, I declare!" Catalina's heart raced. Her breath came in short, hot spurts. "Who could have ever imagined that I would one day stare true ignorance in the face? Oh, but you have proven beyond a shadow of a doubt that it exists, Mr. Monroe! If you feel love is nothing more than another business transaction, then you are even shallower than a woman trying to make a good match."

She wrestled away the arm he still held with one good yank. With one last haughty glare, she turned a slender nose up and spun on her heels. She had only taken one step when she felt his vicelike grip on her once again. Would this nightmare ever end?

"Ah, now I'll get a taste of that feisty Italian temper I've heard so much of." Ben leaned towards Catalina, a snarl of superiority on his lips. His hot breath fanned her face. "Although, I think it might be in my better interest if we involved Harrington in our little ordeal. I can't have you running off and telling your folks wild tales. Can I?"

Catalina attempted to put some space between them and stepped back, brushing up against the horse that stood behind her.

Adrenaline rushed through her veins. Fear. Anger. Humiliation. The emotions swirled through her brain in a violent rush. What could she do? Ben pressed in on her, and she turned her face, the smell of horseflesh strong. Ben's hands began to wander to forbidden regions, and she let out a sharp cry.

The sudden noise caused the horse to dance, and the something pushed into Catalina.

The whip!

She jerked it out of the horse's saddlebag, raised it, and brought it down full-force.

Ben shrieked with pain, his hands holding his face as he fell to his knees.

Ignoring all aspects of ladylike behavior, Catalina hiked her dress up clear above her knees. She wasn't sticking around this place! Free to mount the dancing beast, his apprehension mirrored her own as she climbed into the saddle.

"Yah! Giddy up," she commanded the animal to take flight. His hoof beats seemed to match the rhythm of her heart as she raced away from the river. The strong wind whipped against Catalina's up do, and her hair fell into her face. She tried to shake them away and heard the thundering sound of horse hoofs from behind.

She glanced over her shoulder. Even with long strands blinding the better part of her vision, she could see that Ben had mounted the second horse and was closing in on her. Terror trickled down her back.

"You insufferable wench," he called out. "I'm gonna' teach you where a woman's place is once I catch hold of you!"

Her assailant pulled up beside her, a visible welt forming from forehead to chin. He reached over and grabbed a hold of her horse's reigns, dragging them to a stop.

Catalina raised her whip again, determined to make a stand, but Ben was ready this time. He shielded his face from the blow.

Instead of hitting him in the face, though, Catalina brought the whip down on the horse's shank. The surprised animal bucked, his front legs arching in anger at the unexpected blow.

Having loosened his grip on the reigns to protect himself, Ben lost all control over the horse. Tossed into the air, he flipped over backwards – only a sharp cry sounding out before he landed face-first, in a dismantled heap behind his horse.

"Serves you right," Catalina couldn't help yelling down at Ben in victory. "Next time you'll think twice before assaulting a lady – especially this one! So don't you ever think to threaten me again. I'm not someone to be toyed with, Mr. Monroe!"

Catalina waited for her attacker to reply – for some witty response to her gloating.

Nothing.

Moving her horse closer to the still body, Catalina grimaced at the sight of his limbs sprawled in unnatural positions. The sight of a bone protruding out of a leg elicited a gasp.

She sat momentarily, biting her lower lip while she thought about what she should do. Ben had just threatened her, so why should she help him? Torn between the decision to stay or go, she finally decided that the Good Samaritan wouldn't abandon an enemy. How could she?

Carefully sliding off her horse, she made small half steps before closing the gap between herself and the crumpled body. She wouldn't leave him lying there if his injuries were serious.

"Ben? Are you all right?" Catalina waited a brief moment for a response.

Still nothing.

She grabbed one of his arms. "Come on," she said and pulled him onto his back. He turned over, his head rolling about in a lazy fashion, his eyes two dull orbs void of any life.

Catalina felt the blood drain from her face as she stared at his lifeless one.

Then her world fell away.

Chapter Three

Matthew Martin couldn't believe this grim shadow was the same girl he had seen at the picnic a few hours earlier. She sat in a chair, her chin in one slender hand; a once proud back slumped as though she held the weight of the world on her shoulders.

What exactly had happened out in those woods? Could he have saved her from the ordeal if he had bid a little higher on her lunch? And why hadn't he continued the bid anyway? He certainly could have afforded it.

He already knew the answer, though.

His heritage.

While plenty of folks accepted the fact that he was half Mexican, others in town still looked at him like he would rob the bank at any moment. It was as though the part he played in the capture of some of Pancho Villa's men meant nothing. The deputy badge he wore made little difference in the face of prejudice.

He let out an irritated snort, snagging Catalina's attention. She studied him, their gazes connecting for several beats. Then her eyes squinted with defiance, and she hiked that pretty nose and turned away.

Great! She must think I'm judging her.

Matthew wanted to go over and explain himself. He knew what it was like to be judged without all the facts. Besides, he highly doubted Catalina was to blame in all this mess. The Monroe family reminded Matthew of his father's kin. Rich and always right – people with power didn't usually get to the top without climbing on the backs of others. He had learned that the first time his father turned him away.

What was her story? Her family wasn't the wealthiest, but they were still doing well. Catalina's appearance professed as much. At least, it had at the picnic. The cheerful satin number she sported had been soiled; her green satin stained and the cream laces torn. Stylish leather boots, now caked in mud, peeked out from under an unraveling hem.

She looked helpless.

Looks could be deceiving, though. After all, hadn't the Santé's sent their only daughter to a progressive college for girls?

Still, all that education and liberation and – *who knows what all they teach in a school like that?* – and Catalina wore a look of misery. Matthew grimaced at the sadness that surrounded the girl. Maybe he should offer some sort of comfort.

Ha!

One look at her parents disapproving faces, and he knew they wouldn't appreciate that. Besides, he was only here on official, a witness while Sheriff McBride questioned the young woman.

But maybe a word of condolence?

Matthew nearly stepped forward to say as much when Mrs. Santé abruptly spoke.

"Will someone please bring this girl a cup of tea," she demanded. Both the cook and maid had been actively entertained as they watched their mistress pace a hole in the floor. However, now they were both sent scurrying towards the kitchen. "Bring one for me, as well. I need something to calm my nerves."

"Yes. Tea for everyone is probably a good idea," Mr. Santé chimed in. "Then maybe Catalina will be a little more coherent and we'll understand exactly what's going on."

"I already told you a dozen times." Catalina's tired voice had grown hoarse. She shifted in her seat, rubbing the spots where obvious bruises had begun to form.

Why weren't her parents listening?

To make things worse, the sheriff insisted that she recap how a woman with little more strength and virility than a petite girl could manage to unhorse a grown man.

"Yes, we all heard you," Sheriff McBride replied in a thick Southern drawl. "That's why I sent a couple of deputies with Doc Meade. Maybe he'll find young Monroe badly bruised instead of…"

Dead.

The unspoken word hung in the thick air, a heavy drape of bad omens.

"Yes, well, what I don't understand is how you've even managed to land yourself in this position, Catalina." Mrs. Santé had gone from pacing the room to sitting beside her daughter, wringing nervous hands as she fretted. "You know very well that you should have never been with that man – *any* man – without a chaperone. And in such a secluded place! Didn't you think of your reputation even a little?"

"I thought he was going to propose." Her explanation sounded weak. Had she questioned the man, or had the scoundrel not given her a choice?

"If he had intended to propose marriage, then he would have come to me first and asked for your hand." Gian Carlos' accent became thick with outrage.

"I'm sorry." The weak apology was all Catalina could manage to get out before Rosie re-entered the room, and placed the tea in front of her young mistress. She offered a smile, but Catalina only hung her head.

Gian Carlos dismissed the maid with a mere nod. As she opened the door to leave, Doctor Meade rushed in. Behind him was a loud commotion.

"I thought it only right to inform Mister Monroe of his son's misfortune. Never would I have thought he'd—"

"I demand justice," Douglas Monroe pushed past the doctor, nearly knocking him over in the process. "There she is! Arrest that murderess at once," he ordered the deputies who followed behind him.

"Now wait a minute," Gian Carlos crossed the room in a matter of seconds to stand in front of his daughter.

"Why, you—" The older Monroe grabbed a hold of Gian Carlos' tie, a fist ready to rain down on the man.

Matthew's pistol flashed in front of the two angry fathers, and the sheriff stepped forward. He motioned for Matthew to lower his weapon.

"There ain't no one goin' to jail. From what I've gathered, Miss Santé was simply defendin' herself."

Mister Monroe tried to interrupt, but the sheriff raised a hand to silence him. "That don't mean to say she won't stand trial. The courts will be open tomorrow. She can go in front of the judge then. In the meantime, I think it should be just fine if Miss Santé spent the night in the confines of her own home, seein' that she really don't have no other place to go."

"But she could escape," Douglas countered.

"To where?" The sheriff scoffed.

Mr. Monroe huffed, then silence settled over the room.

"Exactly. Her family, friends and community ties are all here. I feel pretty confident that a cold, hard jail cell is unnecessary for this little lady. Besides, Douglas, you should be more concerned with whether or not her accusations 'bout your son's recent dealings are true. If that be the case, your family's gonna' have a lot more worries than I think y'all really want."

Douglas Monroe turned ripe red as the sheriff ordered him out of the Santé home. The doctor followed suit, the deputies that had accompanied him trailing close behind.

Matthew smiled, satisfaction warming him that honor had held more weight than dollars. He sobered up when Sheriff McBride addressed Catalina's father.

"Now that I said it was okay for her to remain in your care, I want a solemn vow from you that I can trust you'll do just that. I don't like the idea of having to throw a woman – especially one as young as your daughter – in jail. That don't mean I won't, though."

"Of course." Gian Carlos readily agreed. "You can even have one of your men to keep watch outside. In fact, I think I would rather prefer it after the little scene we've just had."

"Actually, that's a fine idea." Sheriff McBride nodded in agreement. He turned back to Matthew. "Think you can handle it, Deputy?"

Matthew puffed up his shoulders and straightened his back. Finally! After two years, now was his chance to prove a Tex-Mex man was worth his word. That would stop all the niggling about having someone like him working for the law!

"Yes, sir." Matthew approached the men and held out a hand to Gian Carlos. "I promise I'll do a good job protecting your daughter, Mr. Santé."

Gian Carlos looked the deputy up and down, the kind of "sizing up" that usually led to trouble.

For him.

But how could he blame the older gent? He would have acted much the same if he had a daughter. So he clamped his jaw and remained silent, his face an expressionless mask as the man finished his inspection.

"I believe you will, Deputy."

Catalina rolled for at least the hundredth time and flopped one sore arm out, her hand landing on something soft. Something not the mattress.

She forced heavy eyelids open, flickering and finally focusing on the object under her hand. Oh, that's right. Her Bible. She had fallen asleep, reading. Running her fingers down the smooth black leather, a small twinge of guilt settled in. How long had it been since she opened it of her own accord? Hoping to find some comfort, she had scoured the pages until her eyes landed on a timeless passage in one of the gospels. Replaying the words of John 8:32 in her mind, she'd finally drifted off into a restless slumber.

Would the truth really set her free? One of Ben's accusations stuck out more than anything else, burning into her consciousness.

Do you think you're some good little Christian...?

She fingered the gold lettering on the cover, memories painting a sad picture. Ben was right.

She had attended mostly just to make a good match and marry into the Monroe family. She could hardly recall any of the sermons – most of the reverend's words had been muffled amongst the daydreams of what her wedding would be like. Then there were the imaginings of what married life had in store for her. When she sang hymns, they weren't really heartfelt. If anything, she had sung solely to showcase her voice. And college? She hadn't even tried to find a church home. A few girls had invited her to go to services, but Cat had always made an excuse about an errand needing to be done. After a while, the girls stopped asking Catalina to do anything at all with them. Of course, she hadn't minded much as she had been more interested in taking in all the sights the state's capitol had to offer. Sitting through boring church services with grumpy old men who droned on and on about eternal suffering for the wicked paled in comparison to rallies against injustice.

Catalina let out a tormented sob and buried her head into her pillow as though she could hide from the shame. No wonder Benjamin had thought she was as worldly as he. She had fooled herself into thinking that she was an exemplary Christian because she tried to be a good person, volunteering in the soup kitchen or assisting her mother with whatever charity case the women's knitting circle took up. Her mother had touted "faith without works is dead" so much that she had created a routine to be a "good Christian" – without ever truly coming to know God! He had been little more than a prayer at mealtimes or the subject of Sunday sermons.

An intense desire to know just what a person had to do to become a true Christian took root in her belly. But who could she ask? Certainly not her parents. They would be shocked to think their daughter had never come to know the Lord, as would anyone else within their circle of friends. The only person she could really think of was Reverend Livingstone. Surely he wouldn't judge her.

It's his job to lead people to salvation, she reasoned with herself as she crawled out of bed and padded barefoot to the window. She pulled the heavy drapes back and peered into the pitch black night. Frustration gnawed at her insides.

Not even a hint of sunlight on the horizon, but what did she expect? The last chimes she recalled hearing from the old grandfather clock in the hall made it little more than two o'clock in the morning. The hours slowly ticked away like a countdown of what would follow in the morning. Would she go to jail forever? Who would snap shut the cell door? The deputy who stood watch downstairs? Was he really guarding her… or judging her like everyone else?

The bedroom door flew open, startling Catalina. The drapes fell back into place.

"Good. You're awake." Teresa Santé marched into the room and the maid scurried in behind her, seemingly infused with the understanding that her typically lackadaisical manner in doing things would not be tolerated in the least.

"Mother! What—"

"Now, keep in mind what we talked about, Rosie." Ms. Santé stared pointedly at the maid. "Pack the items as listed earlier and notify me the moment the bags are in the car."

Pack? Bags? Catalina found her voice when she saw the maid put her silver brush and mirror into her valise. "Why is Rosie packing my things?"

"Never you mind. Put this on and come down to the study." Her mother thrust a gown against her chest, barely waiting for her to grasp the material before bustling out the door.

Her traveling dress? Catalina held it out in front of her, staring at the ugly charcoal fabric. She had only worn it twice, for traveling to and from the college campus. Sturdy and made in a fashion to keep a body warm; designed to ward off unwanted attention.

Catalina shuddered, but didn't waste any time donning the hideous dress. Why was Mama up and about so early, and where were they going?

At the open doorway, she scanned her quarters, an anxious, unsettled feeling coating her belly. What was she leaving behind? And when would she return? Something didn't feel right.

Rosie pushed past her without so much as muttering an apology and Catalina turned to follow suit, but the soft leather of her Bible snagged her attention. She scooped it up and tried to force it into the pocket of her traveling dress, but it hung halfway out. So, she clutched it to her chest instead and raced down the stairs, dread swelling up like rising floodwaters.

She paused outside the study. Who – or what – was waiting for her behind the closed doors? Breathing a silent prayer for courage, she forced herself to turn the knob, the old hinges complaining with a soft, rusty sigh. Catalina cringed as she crept into the room. A large oak desk flanked one corner, with two leather armchairs in front of it. A matching davenport sat across from it with an oval glass table to accommodate luncheons, a cheery fire glowing from the hearth. It failed to do its job, though. Was the chill in the air from her parents' odd behavior? They stood in front of the fireplace, their voices soft murmurs against the crackling flames.

What, or who, were they discussing? Catalina swallowed the lump of dread snowballing in her throat and stepped closer, the heels of her shoes barely making a sound. She wrapped unsteady arms around her stomach. Had the judge called for her already? A whimper escaped her mouth before she could stop it.

She didn't know what was in store for her, but she was certain that life as she knew it was about to change forever.

Chapter Four

"Catalina, dear." Her mother rushed over and tugged her arm towards the settee. "Why don't you have a seat with me?"

As both ladies took a seat on the settee, Gian Carlos pulled one of the armchairs closer to the sofa. He rubbed his face with his hands as if he could wake himself from a nightmare. Finally he sighed, speared her with haunted eyes, and spoke. "I once knew a young Mexican man who dreamed of living in America and becoming a fine business owner. However, his father had different plans for him. The father wanted him to settle down and take over running his ranch. Now, the son didn't mind the settling down part one bit. He already had a special señorita whom he planned to marry. But the idea of being a farmer all his life went against everything the son desired. He told his father as much. The old man was furious. He shouted that if the land he wanted to leave his son wasn't good enough, then the son wasn't good enough to inherit the land. He went on to tell his son that if he left for America, then he might as well consider himself disowned. The son knew that to be true when on the day of the wedding, all the townsfolk came to witness the exchange of vows – except the father. The son searched the crowd, but the old man was nowhere to be seen. Furious that his father would humiliate him and disrespect his young bride, the son packed his horse and wagon with their clothes and a few meager provisions. Together, he and his new wife made their way to America."

Gian Carlos paused to look at her, his gaze intense. "Do you understand what I'm telling you?"

"I guess. I mean, I understand the story although I don't understand *why* you're telling it to me."

Taking a deep breath, Gian Carlos finally told his daughter the truth. "Catalina, I was that young man."

She stared at her father for a long moment. Who was this stranger? Her head jerked to her mother, seeking confirmation.

"No! That's not true." A myriad of reasons flitted through her mind. "It can't be! We're Italian. I mean... All the little sayings, and the way we live. I know all the stories about your villa and my crazy Uncle Adamo."

"No, child. Those are the real lies." Teresa hung her head. "While we do have Spanish ancestors, we made up the whole story about being Europeans from Italy. We had no choice when we saw how badly Mexicans were being treated as we crossed International Boulevard. In fact, we were right outside of Sonora when we witnessed an entire family attacked. It was terrible! No different from today with all the problems on the *frontera*." Her mother looked at her husband and held out a hand.

Catalina saw the tender exchange, but could only marvel at the sound of the Spanish her mother had spoken. It was so similar to the Italian word for border – *frontiera*. A lilt in their accented English, a tweaking of customs. What had it taken for her parents to claim another culture? Two, really.

Catalina frowned.

Her whole life… was a lie?

Her father folded his wife's hand in his and nodded, encouraging her to continue.

"After a few bad business dealings, we knew we'd never be treated fairly. So we took the little money we had made, and decided to get as far away from Texas as we could."

"We caught a carriage that was traveling east," Catalina's father interrupted. "There was already an old Italian onboard – a businessman. He was an exciting sort of character and he loved to talk - mostly about himself. He told us all about his life, his country - he even taught us some Italian phrases. Oh, he was so proud of his heritage! He was even prouder of his accomplishments, though. He said he was heading to Charlotte, North Carolina to run a mercantile he had won in a game of cards. Then he invited me to work for him! He didn't care about where we came from – just wanted 'good people' working for him." At the sound of a soft knock on the door, Gian Carlos paused. "Yes?"

The door swung open.

"The bags are in the carriage, sir."

"Thank you, Rosie. Please bring in the tea."

The young maid hesitated, concern painting her face before she curtsied and took her leave.

Gian Carlos was either oblivious to the maid's apprehension or simply didn't care. Either way, he continued on with his story.

"We traveled for nearly two months, making several stops along the way. We agreed to work for him, and the man became our employer, a *patron*. We accompanied him everywhere he went. And I learned nearly everything about our Italian companion. We joked and got on well, enjoyed many laughs at my

pitiful attempts to speak Italian and his equally sad
endeavor of speaking Spanish. We were becoming such
good friends, and it looked like we would all have a
very nice life here in Charlotte." Gian Carlos let out a
sigh and continued, "It was not to be, though."

Teresa's breath caught and a hand fluttered up to
her chest. Her eyes fluttered closed and she murmured a
soft prayer. The reverent words forced Catalina
forward, her interest piqued as to what had happened to
the old man.

"We were crossing into Carolina territory when we
heard gunfire. The horseman must have been shot first,
because the carriage veered off the road and fell on its
side. Your mother was knocked unconscious when I
landed on top of her. I was so busy trying to awaken her
that I didn't even realize that Adamo had begun to
climb out of the coach. I guess he intended to
investigate or maybe just run away. I don't know what
was going through his mind. All I know is that a second
shot rang out and beside me fell my new friend – a
bullet to his head. I heard footsteps outside the carriage
just as your mother was coming to. I threw myself back
on top of her and covered her mouth when she moaned.
I told her to play dead and we both just lay there for the
longest time. Finally I heard the footsteps leaving as
some man spoke aloud that the crash must've killed the
others in the carriage – us, that is."

"I think I can guess the rest," Catalina interrupted
her father as the maid entered once again. As if that
could derail her father's confession, or change the clock
back to a time when the most important concern of the
day revolved around who was winning the war.

Rosie placed the tea on the table and left the room,
her eyes averted.

Catalina studied the door as it closed, the absence of a click hardly noticeable. "Since you knew where the store was, you decided to take it over."

She had tried to hide the disappointment, but her voice was dripping with it.

"In a matter of speaking, yes." Gian Carlos turned away from her. "I didn't just dig through a dead man's belongings and take the deed to the store, though. Surely God had a purpose, allowing us to meet and for things to unfold the way they did. The man's name was Adamo Santé – a bizarre coincidence we joked about when I first introduced myself as a Santiago. So when he passed, I chose to honor of the old Italian – a man who had given us a chance when few others would. I adopted his name. No longer Carlos Santiago, I became Gian Carlos Santé, Adamo's brother. Your mother took the last name as well and we've been the Santé family ever since."

So even her last name was a lie. Would she ever recognize the truth again? A sour taste filled her mouth. Why were they telling her this, and why now? "Didn't anyone catch on that you weren't exactly Italian?"

"It told ourselves it was the truth in some ways." Her father defended the decades-old choice they had to make. "We come from a region of Mexico where the people look more European than the native Indian tribes found there. I suppose that's the one thing that can be credited to the Spanish conquistadors who ruled the country during the sixteenth century – some of them your mother's family. So it was never a lie when we told you we were of European blood. Aside from that, we spoke English fairly well. Coupled with a few Italian phrases that we had learned from Adamo, everyone accepted that I was Gian Carlos Santé, born of

Milan - who would be caring for the store in his brother's stead. Your mother had a little harder time with the language. So she claimed she was Spanish due to her heritage." Gian Carlos pleaded his case. "It wasn't a lie! Her great-grandfather had been a general in the Spanish army. So it really gave us an opportunity to still embrace some of our customs and teach our children Spanish."

"Not that it did much good." Catalina thought about her the broken languages she spoke. A drop of Italian, a smidgeon of Spanish. Not enough of either language to make useful conversation. She shook her head in disbelief. Not that it mattered any. All the lies that had been told equated to something far worse. They were Mexican. Not Italian. Not even Spanish.

Mexican!

That meant she was, too.

She rolled the idea around in her mind and cringed. There had been more than one occasion on which she had thought badly about the country and its entire people – namely after Pancho Villa's attack on Columbus. Now which country she was supposed to pledge her allegiance to?

She shook away the idea and considered her father's story. There were still some loose ends to it.

"And how did you explain your supposed brother's lasting absence from the store he never claimed?" Catalina questioned her father. "Didn't anyone think it strange that he never showed up to take over?"

"A few of the local gossips did begin to question me after a while. At first, I told them that I didn't know what was keeping him and that I was waiting for correspondence. I began to worry because it felt like we had built one lie on top of another. I thought it was going to catch up with us." Gian Carlos looked panged with guilt. "At the same time, I couldn't risk losing the store and everything we had worked so hard for. You see, it was right around that time we found out your mother was expecting your brother, Gabriel. So, I was in a real quandary. I didn't want to lie anymore, but I didn't want to tell everyone that I had mislead them."

"We were just beginning to fit into society." Her mother chimed in. "Our lives had become so pleasant. Then we thought about the baby – really, any children God blessed us with. So we did what we felt was right."

Gian Carlos had stood up and began pacing. The air was heavy with anticipation as they waited for him to continue. "And that was when I came to know God."

Catalina perked up.

"How did you come to know Him?" She didn't want to admit it, but the truth was that she was interested in learning how she could do the same. Not just for name's sake, but to *really* come to know him. However, telling her parents that she had never been saved brought shame to her cheeks. She turned an ear to her father.

"We had been attending church services for a couple of months - the same we all go to now. At that time, we only had traveling preachers who would stop by every other Sunday. One of them ministered to the congregation so tenderly. He spoke of how we could each reach deliverance just by praying to God that we accepted Jesus Christ as our Savior, and asking Him to forgive us for our sins. Then he invited anyone who was willing to approach the altar and receive Christ as their savior. I was so moved and wanted to step forward, but I couldn't. I was so embarrassed at the thought that your mother would think badly of me. I was embarrassed of what she would think if she knew that I had never accepted God before."

A soft smile touched her mother's face. "Yet, I thought the same as your father. It wasn't until I had gone out for my evening stroll that I myself came to know Christ."

"For me, it was the next morning right before I opened the store," Gian Carlos confessed. "I kept thinking about how I couldn't face telling another lie if anyone asked about our situation. That's when I turned to God. I admitted to Him that I felt like a horrible sinner for taking advantage of an opportunity when I saw it. Then I asked God to give me the right words to say if anyone questioned about Adamo."

"Did it work?" The salvation stories of her parents resonated with Catalina's own feelings.

If prayer worked for them, then maybe it'll work for me too.

"It did," her father smiled happily. "When one of the old-timers came in, he casually asked how much longer they'd be seeing my face around – not that he minded any. I was fair with all the customers and he wanted to know if he could expect the same from Adamo."

"What did you tell him?"

"The truth. I said that Adamo had suffered an extremely bad accident while traveling by coach to take over the store and that, due to his passing, I would remain the permanent owner of Santé's Mercantile. The old man offered his condolences, paid for his purchase and went on his way. I suppose he must have related the information to others, because very few ever questioned me about Adamo again."

"But I'm your daughter. Why didn't you tell me the truth before? And why now?" How could her father withhold such valuable information? Her name, their livelihood, their heritage! Lies! All of it!

Her father hung his head as though defeated.

His wife came to his rescue. "We didn't tell you or your brother because it didn't seem of much consequence to know." She explained. "When a school assignment required that Gabriel write about his heritage, we had him write about how he was a child of God – instead of flesh and blood family members. He received perfect marks, too. In fact, the teacher - Mrs. O'Neal, I believe – said she found the paper inspiring. Incidents like that one just seemed to unfold by themselves. We thought that surely it had been God's will."

"All right." Catalina tried to mask her irritability, but a frustrated sigh managed to escape all the same. "I understand that you felt that a couple of children couldn't keep such a secret to themselves. That still doesn't explain why you've decided to tell me this in the wee hours of the morning." That feeling of dread had started to rise up again and stuck like a lump in her throat. She clenched the Bible to her chest, as if the truth inside its pages could protect her from the horrific facts just revealed.

"We're not going to watch our daughter hang from a tree just because of an accident." A thin grimace stretched across her father's face. "You will go to Mexico and stay with your grandfather until we can straighten out this mess."

"What!" Catalina's cup rattled against the saucer, the dark liquid jostling over the edges and staining the front of her dismal gown. She bolted away from the couch. "I am not going anywhere – especially not Mexico. I am INNOCENT!" She emphasized the last word with enough force to carry her voice throughout the house.

"We know you are, darling," her father soothed, reaching out a gentle hand as he approached her. "However, we fear what Mr. Monroe will do to persuade the judge to his way of thinking. You wouldn't believe the things he's been saying around town. He's definitely a man out for blood, and with the kind of money and power he has – well, it wouldn't be too hard for him to get what he wants. Why, I've already gotten word from several regulars who have claimed they couldn't possibly be patrons any longer."

What? The town was siding against her family? How could that be? "But surely he understands it was an accident. I was in love with Ben." Had she been in love with Ben? Really? She didn't know anymore. And especially not after his revelation. How much more hadn't he told her? Still, she could never intentionally kill *anyone*. She shook her head in confusion. "Why would I want to purposely hurt him?"

"Sweet child," Her mother stood and rushed over to her daughter. She embraced Catalina, holding her daughter close to her. "Mr. Monroe doesn't care about what really happened. For him, it's 'an eye for an eye' kind of situation."

Catalina pulled away from her mother and stared at both parents.

Her mother swiped away silent tears with a tissue, not meeting Catalina's gaze. Her father's face was firm, unyielding.

No hope there. So this was how it was to be. She would be carted off to some strange country where people didn't even speak English while everything and everyone she knew was left behind.

"When will I leave?" she asked, choking back sobs that threatened to betray her voice.

"With God's grace, you'll be gone before the morning comes."

God's grace?

Catalina's mind reeled. How could any of this horrible situation be favorable in His eyes?

Chapter Five

Matthew Martin glanced around the cozy parlor, still unsure why he had been offered coffee at such an early hour of the morning. Looking down, he marveled at the small cup that warmed his hands. It seemed like a toy in his large palms, again reminding him of how much he looked like his father. No wonder the mean dog had been able to run him off so easily all those years back!

Well over six feet and with a scowl that could turn a sinner into a saint, women in town had the tendency to cross the street when Matthew stormed down the sidewalk. One even ducked into a shop and peered out the blind slats until he passed! That's why he was nearing thirty and had yet to settle down. It wasn't the badge – like some of the other deputies liked to joke. He liked working for the law, but could easily give it up for the right gal. He just hadn't found one that wouldn't scare off. That is, until he met Catalina.

The first time he noticed her was at her mother's dress shop. He had wanted to send something to his mother for her birthday, and the pretty dress displayed in the front window seemed appropriate. He was surprised to enter the store and hear an old childhood tune waft towards him. Following the rich hum, he walked around one of the aisles and found Catalina. She was arranging a spool of fabric on one of the shelves –

the wordless Mexican ballad soft on her lips. He wanted to ask her how she knew the song, but an older woman interrupted.

"Can I help you with something?" The woman measured him, a wary look in her eyes.

Distrust. Suspicion.

He'd seen it before. Lots of times. "Um, yes, actually. I was interested in the blue gown in the front window. In fact, I was just about to ask your employee for assistance."

"*Mi hija* has a previous order to fill." The look in the woman's eyes needed no voice. Her daughter was unavailable.

"Yes, ma'am." Matthew gritted, his teeth clenched in anger that he wasn't even good enough for his own kind. Making his purchase, he existed the store – a quick glance over his shoulder catching the girl's playful look. It announced that she had been aware of his presence, a witness to the short exchange.

He stepped outside and stood on the sidewalk, staring into the window for a long minute. That yearning to settle down – to have what he never did growing up – bedded in the pit of his stomach. He studied the sew shop beauty. She held her head high and stood spine-straight, looking ready and capable.

That was one reason he had dared to bid on her lunch pail at the Sunday social. However, the memory of her mother's disapproving scowl is what had stopped him from raising the price any higher. He was supposed to be on duty – just doing his rounds to make sure that peace was kept.

You sure did a great job there.

Matthew shook his head in disgust. He had dropped the ball hard on this one. The fact that it was a girl like him – half Mexican, half American – made him all the more interested. Especially the story he had overheard. He had grown up not knowing his father. But what would it have been like to not know his heritage at all?

He glanced up at Gian Carlos.

"You know, you all got really lucky with the way things worked out. Murder – even accidental – usually lands the suspect in jail. Not saying that it won't once the judge gets here." Matthew felt like a heel for allowing the last little bit to slip out, but wasn't it better for the man to be prepared?

Gian Carlos smiled at his candor. "It had nothing to do with luck." He looked up from his cup and stared Matthew square in the eyes. "It was divine intervention… just like you being here."

"Excuse me?"

Gian Carlos drained his cup before setting it down. He studied Matthew for a moment. "Do you really believe it's coincidental that during our greatest time of need, you just happen to be here? Because I don't believe that at all when considering the facts."

Matthew raised a brow and cocked his head to one side. Maybe it was better to humor his host. "And what facts might those be?"

"That you are very much like my daughter." Gian Carlos paused and waited. "I know your secret." He had barely whispered the words as he leaned over the table but they sounded throughout the room like a gunshot.

Matthew's face hardened – furrowed brows informing the man that he didn't appreciate the direction the conversation was turning. Silence was a much better companion than the assumptions of a desperate business man who was probably willing to say anything to save his daughter.

"I highly doubt you would know any secrets I have. That is, if I had any." Matthew raised his chin in challenge.

"So, are you saying that you're not Mexican?" Gian Carlos measured his words while giving the young deputy a knowing look.

"What are you talking about?" Matthew studied the man, suspicion tugging at the corners of his mind. How much Mr. Santé actually know about him? He had never denied his heritage, but he had never admitted it either. Between his "every man" look and the slight drawl that hung on his tongue, most people assumed Matthew was just some good old cowboy transplanted to the South. Even other deputies he worked with accepted him as part of "the family," always horsing around with him as though he was just another one of the boys. If they knew otherwise, they would probably label him a spy for the German army. Rumors already abounded along the southern border of the two countries joining forces against the United States.

Matthew sat ramrod, a hard look bearing down on Gian Carlos. "I've never said I wasn't Mexican. Just out of curiosity, though, what makes you think I am?"

"My wife says you are."

Matthew looked down into his empty coffee cup. He had wondered if the lady of the house recognized him after their brief encounter in her dress shop. Apparently, she had. More surprising was the fact that she had correctly guessed his heritage. There was no use denying the facts. Besides, he was mildly curious as to where the truth would lead him. He glanced up at Gian Carlos. "How did she know?"

"She said that she spoke to you in Spanish when you were in her dress shop. You didn't act surprised, or question what she said." When Matthew nodded in confirmation, his host continued. "She seems to possess the talent to recognize one of her own countrymen."

"Where y'all from?"

"Michoacán." Gian Carlos sat back, easing into his admission. "My father was one of the ejidos. He spent his days farming the land."

Matthew decided to lay all his cards on the table. "You're sending Catalina to him."

"A father should do everything in his power to save his children." Gian Carlos lifted a thick questioning brow. "Even if it means swallowing his pride, or asking a deputy to break the law."

Matthew straightened. He knew what the man was asking of him. Was it wise to get involved, though? He'd be risking his livelihood. At the same time, it could be his opportunity to get to know Catalina better. Wasn't that the *real* reason he had agreed to guard her anyway? At the same time, he'd be risking his job. Good grits! A lot more than that could happen. He could be risking his own neck.

He studied her father a moment longer, weighing the pros and cons before finally answering.

"What do you want me to do?"

Chapter Six

"Is this really the only way across?" Catalina grimaced as the Model T slowly rolled onto the old boat. Her stomach churned in rhythm with the waves rippling across the Mississippi River. Crossing her arms across her chest, she frowned. How much more could a lady be expected to endure?

"Unfortunately, yes." Matthew eased the car onto the ferry before stealing a quick glance at his charge. She looked the mixture of worn and worried, one hand gripping the car door while the other balled up bunches of her traveling dress. He understood her apprehension and couldn't blame her. He'd rather ride a horse than in one of these new four-wheel contraptions. However, Mr. Santé had insisted his daughter travel in comfort. If only he knew the truth!

The day before had seemed like a never-ending journey of almost nonstop driving until they reached Natchez, Mississippi, a small town without a hotel.

Matthew had asked if there was a room to rent anywhere and they were directed towards the magnificent Dunleith Inn. The site of the large plantation home was obviously a welcomed one.

"Oh, thank Heavens! My prayer has been answered." Catalina had sat forward, her hands on the dash as they rode up the cobbled drive. If her thoughts were anything like his, then she was imagining the servants drawing a hot bath. Ready to sleep like the dead, he couldn't wait to clean up and pass out.

However, Southern hospitality at its finest was the last order of the day.

"I'm sorry, sir. We have no vacancy at the moment." A lanky, beetle-eyed man with oily hair and too-perfect teeth flashed them a false smile, the corners of which never reached his eyes. "The inn is completely booked due to the campaign."

Hot tears mixed with exhaustion began to gather in the corner of Catalina's eyes. "This is completely inexcusable!" She pounded the registration desk with one small fist, her voice threatening to raise the dead themselves.

"Hey, now. It'll be all right." Matthew placed a soft hand on her shoulder and tried to pull her away from the innkeeper who stood paralyzed with apparent shock. "It's sour news, to be sure. Especially after all you've been through. Still, there's no need to get all hot over something out of your control."

Good grits and gravy, who was that speaking? Quick to draw and ask questions later, Matthew could hardly believe the words coming out of his own mouth.

His level-headed kindness caught Catalina's attention, too. Hands dropping to her sides, she turned to face him. His eyes appeared soft with concern, a small frown gathering between his brows. Did he really care about all she had been through? She opened her mouth to speak, but was interrupted by the inn clerk.

"Oh, I couldn't abide to think of you leaving here with a less-than-perfect opinion of our beautiful hotel." The clerk picked up a bell and rang a butler who was ordered to prepare a fine Southern meal at the inn's expense. "Think of it as our way of formally apologizing for any inconvenience. Also, it is our greatest wish that y'all keep us in mind should there be another plan to visit our fair town."

Catalina took some solace in the generous offer, but it still didn't change the facts. She'd be spending the night in the car! Worse yet, she made herself appear like some spoiled, pampered brat in front of Deputy Martin – a thought that made her pause. Why did she care what he thought of her?

"I'm sorry. It's been a rather difficult day." She offered an apology to the innkeeper. "If you'd be so kind as to excuse me, and show me to the wash closet."

"Of course." The man picked up the bell once again, the small tinkling metal producing the butler a second time.

Matthew watched her stroll away, admiring both her assertive walk and quick change in temperament. It took a lot for him to calm down once his tail feathers were ruffled. And to pull it off with some dignity? He nodded with appreciation.

How did she do that anyway?

He was still thinking about how well she had handled the situation when she returned, following the butler who showed them both to the dining room.

"May I?" Remembering the manners his mother had taught him, Matthew pulled out a chair for Catalina.

"Oh, thank you." She sounded surprised as if she hadn't expected him to act so courteous, and awarded him with a brilliant smile. "That's very kind."

Matthew smiled as he took his own seat and the food began to roll out. "Well, what have we got here?" He clapped his hands together and rubbed them.

"It smells delicious." Catalina inhaled deeply as she lowered her head.

Matthew's hands hovered over the bread basket. Was she praying? He shook his head as he plucked out two mouth-watering buttermilk biscuits and slathered them with lemon curd and cream. If she wanted to give thanks to someone, thank the cook! He took stock of the table. Roasted quail, collard greens and sweet tea. The aroma of a few all-time favorites wafted towards him as he took the first bite. Melting back into his chair, a soft moan escaped his chockfull mouth.

Catalina laughed. "Is it that good?"

"Better than manna, I'd wager." Matthew took another bite and watched her pick up a biscuit, the butter knife poised between three dainty fingers. Yep. She was definitely cultured. She savored each dish through a slow, methodical process, never allowing her pinky to touch the food or drinking glass.

"How about we get a couple of these biscuits to bring with us?" she asked.

"My thoughts exactly," Matthew replied and signaled the waiting girl to bring them another bread basket.

They drove to where the Algiers Ferry would cross the Mississippi River and bunkered down for the night – with her *in* the car and him sleeping on the ground beside it. A fact that robbed Catalina of any sleep as she lay wondering about the deputy who lay just a few feet away from her. What was his story? Why did he agree to accompany her? She recalled him bidding on her basket at the lunchbox social. How would that day have turned out if he had been the one to win the bid?

Catalina shook off the thought. Sunlight threatened to spill over the horizon and her sore, dirty body felt to weary to travel any farther. However, rustling from outside alerted her to the fact that Matthew was rearing to go.

"Care for a biscuit?" He spoke through the open window, taking a bite from one of the inn's biscuits, an outstretched hand holding another.

She forced herself upright and accepted his offering.

"Thanks," she replied.

The thought of having to ride a ferry shuttling cars made her feel truly sick. Heat crept up her cheeks, small beads of sweat forming above her brow. What if there was an accident? The thought made her stomach flip.

"These cars must weigh a ton." She took a bite of the cold bread, hoping it would help settle her stomach. What if there's an accident and we sink?"

Matthew climbed into the car, his free hand working the gears as he touched the gas pedal. The ferry had docked and was ready to take on passengers. He registered the concern in her voice, but angry honking from the forming line behind them distracted him.

"Well, now. Weren't you praying last night?" The car rolled forward. He gave an off-handed shrug. "If you believe in God, then you might want to ask that nothing like that happens."

Catalina raised a challenging brow.

"Perhaps I may advise you to do the same."

Matthew waved off her suggestion as he inched the car onto the ferry. "Naw. I'll just allow you to do the praying for both of us. You're sure to be built of a bigger faith."

Catalina's mood quickly changed from fatigued to indignant. She wouldn't stand for yet another man questioning her ability to be a good Christian.

"And just who are you to judge if I'm not, Deputy?" Venom laced each heated word. "Perhaps you don't find much use for God, but that doesn't give you the right to assume others don't measure up. So if you have nothing useful to say, then you should learn to hold your tongue."

"Whoa! Now wait just a minute." Matthew put the vehicle in park and turned around to face his charge. He wasn't sure what had caused the quick attitude change, but he sure as shooting hadn't signed up for a crab fest. "First off, I'm the one who has pretty much sacrificed my job – maybe even my life – to safely see you to your grandfather's home. So, a little appreciation would be nice. Aside from that, I'd much rather prefer if you'd call me by my given name."

Out of everything Matthew said, only one word seemed to catch Catalina's attention.

Sacrifice.

"Sacrifice your life?" Deep ruts furrowed her smooth brow and etched the corners of her eyes. Was she concerned about him? Or just afraid for herself? "Is Mexico really that dangerous?"

How could he have frightened her so? Matthew softened his tone. "That's not how I meant it. I was trying to convey that I was sacrificing my *way* of life. I'll never be able to return to Charlotte – or even all of North Carolina without running into trouble. People will think of me as a traitor. Plus, I could be charged with aiding your escape if your father can't clear your name." He paused for a moment, and studied Catalina. Her doe like eyes, bright with curiosity made him want to open up. Taking a deep breath, he decided to take the plunge and tell her the truth.

"You know, Mexico really isn't all that different from America or North Carolina – or anywhere else, for that matter. You've got your good parts, and then you've got some bad parts."

"How do you know?" Catalina perked up. "Have you been there before?"

"I have." An odd smile turned up a portion of Matthew's mouth. His eyes narrowed and he looked around the car as though he were assuring that no one else was privy to their private conversation – lest his secret be known to the world. "I lived there for the first fifteen years of my life."

Catalina's mouth dropped open, and Matthew couldn't ignore the pretty "o" shape that formed. He forced himself to look back up – focusing on the slight almond contours of her eyes as she spoke." I can't believe you actually *lived* there. What kind of parents would raise their child in such a place? Were they missionaries or something?"

"Actually, my family is a lot like yours – a bit of this mixed with a touch of that. My mother is Mexican; father's American." He smiled at her. "Guess I got the best of both worlds."

"You mean, you're one of them?" Catalina's eyebrows furrowed with disdain, and Matthew watched her expression turn from interest to disgust. He hadn't thought she'd jump for joy to hear he was half-

Mexican, but this reaction was the last thing he expected.

"One of *them*?" That age-old irritation of being prejudged resurfaced. His anger bubbled forth, heat lining each word he clipped out. "What? Did you conveniently forget that you're one of *them*, too?"

As Matthew's voice hardened, so did Catalina's face. There was a small list of things in the world that could be labeled as truly irritating. At the top of that list was the idea of someone speaking down to her. Especially when that person supported bandits like the ones involved in the attack on Columbus, New Mexico. Catalina bit the inside of her cheek before unleashing her own wrath. "My family happens to be of *Spanish* descent. We were brilliant explorers on a quest to conquer new lands."

She lifted her nose two inches higher, daring Matthew to refute her.

"Oh, that's even better – to conquer an entire race by brutal force."

"You know what I mean." Catalina huffed in frustration. "My ancestors weren't savages living in the dirt, sacrificing each other to false gods."

Matthew was quick on the uptake. "You've got that right. They were civilized people acting like savages by killing those weaker than themselves, all in the name of God."

Catalina sputtered, her mounting anger producing a rude snort. If there was anything Matthew Martin knew how to do better than ruffle her feathers, then she couldn't imagine what it might be. Never had anyone proven to be so contrary.

"I think it's better if we just agree that we're not going to see eye to eye on this subject, and leave it at that, *Deputy* Martin." She purposely emphasized his title. "Let's just concentrate on getting to my grandfather's ranch safely, and spare each other the details of our personal beliefs or lives."

Crossing her arms about her chest, Catalina stared out the window, studying the crew as they lined up the Algiers Ferry with four remaining cars.

"Look." Matthew ran a hand through his hair and let out a long sigh. "This isn't exactly how I imagined it would be when I agreed to take you to your grandfather's house."

Catalina turned back to Matthew – her shapely brows again arched, but this time in question. "Well, Deputy, what exactly did you imagine?"

Matthew shifted uneasily. What had he thought would happen? Even he was unsure of his true desires. All he knew was that he had felt an intense urge to help Catalina in any way possible. He looked back at her – a hardly intelligible answer about to tumble out when he was saved by a knock on the car door. Matthew turned to see one of the crewmen motioning for him to sign in.

"I better go put our names on the docket." Matthew decided to try for diplomacy. "Do you want to wait here, or would you care to walk around a bit?"

"I'll get out."

Catalina gathered a small carpetbag carrying some personal effects and her Bible. She placed it under a traveling blanket for safekeeping – sure that few would really be interested in stealing a bag filled with items that held value to no one but to the owner. Readjusting a bobby pin, she pushed back a stubborn stray curl and pinned it back in place.

As Catalina readied herself, Matthew decided to prove his mother hadn't raised him to argue with women. Showing that he did have at least *some* manners, he slid out the driver's side of the car and opened the passenger door.

"Allow me."

The quiet tenderness in his voice surprised Catalina, forcing her to glance up as she took hold of his hand. Gone was the stubborn jaw that she had witnessed only minutes before. His firm features were now softened by compelling blue eyes that beckoned her to trust him. They held her in a trance as she began to rise out of the car. Distracted by the unexpected gesture of kindness, Catalina failed to lift her dress as she climbed out of the backseat. Her heel caught on the hem of her dress and she tumbled out the door.

And right into his arms.

"Oh, I am so sorry." Heat rushed to her face, and the blood began to pound in her temples as he gingerly stood her upright. She felt small as his strong hands lingered momentarily on her waist, causing desire to well up inside her. She stood there breathless. Waiting. Wanting.

Wanting what?

Him.

The sudden realization that she found him attractive unnerved her. A small shiver of fear ran through her.

"No harm done." Matthew jerked back and released her. The absence of his hands around her left her feeling cold and humiliated.

No man on earth would be interested in a murderess.

Not a single one in his right mind. Catalina didn't have the right to a happy life after taking the possibility away from someone else. And how could she find herself attracted to this man – any man, for that matter – after all that just happened? A familiar pain squeezed her heart. With a rigid bend, she forced herself to pick up her bag.

"Yes, well. Thank you all the same." Her words sounded strained even to her own ears. "I think I'll walk around a bit while you take care of business."

"Uh, all right." Matthew hesitated. "I'll be back in a few minutes."

He set a pace away from her as if fire lit his shoes. Better to focus on paying their fare and sign the log than being caught acting amorous. How could he be so careless? She'd already made it crystal clear that she wanted nothing to do with him. After all, he had descended from savages. Right? Matthew shook his head and snorted. She may as well have said he came from monkeys. He may not be the most religious man on the planet, but he did know that God created all men equal.

It was a shame Catalina didn't believe so. She was so proud of her family history – one from so long ago that it held no real importance anymore. Didn't she understand that she was one of them? Disappointment seeped throughout him. He had felt a brief connection between them. At least, he thought he had. The alarm that had stained her delicate features said otherwise. She obviously feared him – or, at least, what he might be capable of doing to her. Or was it just a carryover from her recent attack?

He blew out a sigh. *Leave it alone, Martin!* He shuffled into line behind several other passengers and dug around in the pocket of his faded corduroy pants for his old leather billfold. He fished around for a two-dollar bill. What had he done? Had he ruined his life for the Santé family?

Catalina thought back to the beginning of her travels as she watched Matthew line up with other passengers, his tall, black-clad figure stiffened by whatever thoughts consumed him.

She had felt an odd mixture of excitement and uncertainty when her father introduced Matthew as the one to take her to her grandfather's ranch. Satisfied to finally learn the name of her mysterious bidder, yet nervous that they were fleeing in the middle of the night. The idea that he was a lawman hadn't soothed her fears until she witnessed his unwavering demeanor of calm strength.

Now doubt crept into her mind once more.

Catalina walked toward the port side of the boat and leaned slightly forward in time to catch a surging wave crash against the side. Her disposition matched the dark water. Closing her eyes, she breathed in deeply, imagined the strong surf washing over her – the fierce current cleansing her foul mood. She sent up a small prayer of thanks for the moment of peace.

"Careful now."

Catalina gasped as a hand tightened around her arm and pulled her back. She looked up at the stranger who interrupted her moment of tranquility. His face looked worn and dangerous – or maybe it was just the ugly, jagged scar that ran down his left cheek. Whatever the reason, his neatly combed blonde hair and fashionably tailored suit did little to ease Catalina.

"It'd be a real pity to lose such a pretty little gal to the great Mississippi. Don't you think?" There was something sinister in his proud Southern drawl. His hand stayed on her arm, his thumb caressing her soft flesh.

Catalina grimaced as she pulled herself free. "Thank you for your concern, sir." Her voice offered a token of gratitude, but surely her face belied the aversion she felt for the stranger.

An unpleasant smirk touched the man's lips – his tongue flicking out to moisten them. The small act left Catalina feeling as though she were improperly dressed. She wrapped her arms around herself.

Distracted by something behind her, the man simply nodded. "My pleasure, Miss." He briefly touched his hat. Then he turned, a brisk walk in his heel.

"Who was that?"

Startled, Catalina turned back around. Thankful to see it was Matthew, Catalina gave him a genuine smile. "Oh, it's you."

Matthew raised a quizzical brow. "Of course, it's me. Were you expecting someone else?"

"No, no. It's just…"

Catalina angled over a shoulder, but the stranger was already gone. She shook her head.

"Nothing. I'm just a little spooked about crossing this river." Catalina dismissed the disturbing stranger as simply one of those eccentric sorts that – having obviously come from money –thought he was entitled to letch over women. "I'm fine. Really."

"Well, don't worry. It'll be over in about fifteen minutes."

"Really? I would have thought it takes a lot longer to cross such a large river."

"Not this particular area we're crossing." Matthew pointed across the river to the landing dock in the horizon. "The boat will pull in right about there."

Catalina bit her lip while she digested that bit of information. The dock looked welcoming, and they would be halfway to their destination once they reached it. What would that would mean for Matthew? What would he do once he got to Mexico? Would he stick around? After all, he was from there.

It would be nice to have a familiar face around.

Why would he, though? After the way she had behaved, he would probably just drop her off at her grandfather's ranch and be on his way. Besides, it wasn't like she really wanted him around. Right?

Catalina tilted her head and studied him.

He was now leaning over the side of the boat the same as she had. However, he didn't look like he was dreaming about drowning his sorrows in the churning waters below. Instead he was staring at the opposite shore with a pensive look.

"A penny for your thoughts?" Catalina regretted asking almost as soon as the words were out. The less she knew about him, the better. Right?

Continuing to lean against the side, Matthew gave her a once-over.

He decided to have a little fun with her.

"Only a penny? Is that what people are charging nowadays? Not me. My thoughts are worth a whole nickel." The laughter in his tone danced in his playful eyes, their brilliance shining like blue gems. A slow, infectious grin spread across Matthew's face. He looked like a mischievous little boy who was trying to buy his way out of trouble after being caught with his hand in the cookie jar.

Catalina bit her lip in a desperate attempt to remain serious, but it was of little use.

Charmed by her softened features, Matthew took a slow step towards her. He raised a tentative hand and pushed back a curl that had worked its way loose.

Catalina's breath stilled as the light touch of his fingers slowly trailed along her cheek. Her beautiful eyes and full mouth were almost irresistible, and he wondered if she tasted as sweet as she looked.

Unasked questions blazed from his eyes, making the cage that she was trying to construct around her heart unhinge. The sudden attraction hit her hard. She forced herself to look away and break the spell. Falling for her escort was not part of the plan.

"Look!" Catalina pointed towards the bank. "We're just about there."

"Then I guess we best get back to the car." Disappointment laced his words. She didn't have any romantic notions about him, so he best leave it at just friends.

No more goo-goo eyes.

"It shouldn't take too long to get it started." He picked up the conversation again as he paced back to the car with a determined step. "It's warm out. So she doesn't need to be cranked or anything."

Catalina questioned his sudden change in mood. She was grateful at the flow of normal conversation between them. Still, it felt like something was suddenly missing. "Well, I suppose that's a good thing." She plodded along behind him, dissatisfied when they reached the Model T.

He took her hand and helped her up and into the front seat. "Shouldn't I ride in the—"

"You'll get a better view of things while we're driving from up here." He cut her off, patting the hood of the car for emphasis – a friendly grin that promised an exciting ride. After all, it was a long trip to Nogales. "Besides, it'll be more fun."

More fun? Hmmm…more trouble maybe. Definitely more dangerous.

Chapter Seven

"Let's see. That covers childhoods, educations, family, friends and dreams." Catalina ticked off all the subjects they had discussed since disembarking the Algiers Ferry. "And there are still so many more topics just waiting to be explored!"

Matthew laughed at her enthusiasm. After coaxing Catalina into joining him on the bench seat, he had begun the drive by playing a spying game with her. One would think of something seen during the drive, and the other person would guess what it was one clue at a time. Some of the objects had elicited interest. Others brought forth moments of mirth. Matthew smiled as he recalled the tinkling melody of her laughter harmonizing with his deeper ones. As the game died down, they found themselves in an easy conversation about everything and anything.

"You're right." He flashed a mischievous look at her. "The car will run out of gas before you do."

Catalina cried out in protest. "Deputy Martin! You were the one picking my brain from the moment the engine turned over."

Another rich, throaty laugh escaped before he could corral it. "How many times do I have to tell you to call me by my first name?"

Catalina's stomach responded before she could. "Oh, excuse me." She wrapped her arms around her midsection, her face turning red-hot as her belly continued to complain.

Matthew glanced over, enjoying the crimson blush that pinked her cheeks. "I'm a bit hungry myself. Nine hours with little more than last night's leftovers doesn't provide enough fuel to keep going." He nodded as he spoke his plans aloud. "It's getting dark, too. So it might be a good idea to stop for the night anyway."

"I pray we're able to find a hotel this time." Catalina didn't include that she looked forward to a nice bath even more than a soft bed. Two days without bathing left her feeling anything but fresh.

"It shouldn't be too difficult." Matthew held out a small handwritten map. "I believe Abilene's only a couple of miles."

"I've only traveled around the Carolinas. I've never been to Texas before." Catalina stared out the window at the changing scenery. The lush trees that previously lined the land in thick groves grew progressively scant. What kind of accommodations they would find amongst the dust and sagebrush. "Will they have a hotel?"

"Most definitely. They have the Windsor Hotel, and it is almost guaranteed to have a room available."

"I assume they have a dining room, too?"

"One of the best. If you thought that ham dinner was good eating last night, then you're in for a real treat today." Matthew smacked his lips as though he could already taste the sizzling steak he had every intention of ordering. The playacting started another round of light laughter.

The merriment died off as the car entered Abilene. The dusty outskirt roads had changed into paved streets, the new black asphalt still glimmering under the hot sun.

"There's the hotel." Matthew motioned ahead to a long, squared building of red brick with several people milling around out front.

"It looks different than any other I've seen before." Only two stories high, but it held a row of ten windows that ran lengthwise. "Although, I *am* used to seeing a mix of cars and buggies parked together." She gave a polite nod to a stranger tying up his team of horses as Matthew parked the car beside them.

Catalina gathered up her skirt. No way was she falling to anyone's arms again! She pushed open the car door and climbed down from the Model T, smiling triumphantly when her feet hit the ground. Turning to retrieve her bag, Matthew reached around her.

"I'll take that." Reaching for the valise, he brushed against her. Catalina's breath caught, the sound of which forced him to straighten quickly. He stared down, allowing the silence to linger for a moment. But only a moment. There was no need to get all swoony for no good reason. He cleared his throat. "Let's check in before they run out of rooms. We wouldn't want a repeat of last night."

Catalina lowered her head in embarrassment as she thought of her behavior the night before. "Well, I did procure a rather nice basket of food for the road."

Matthew simply lifted a questioning brow. The somber look on his face declared he preferred to avoid another incident.

"Oh, alright." Catalina locked her hands in front of her, trying to look innocent. "I promise to be on my best behavior."

Matthew rewarded her with a half-smile and nodded. He jerked his head towards the hotel, and she was quick to pass through the door he held open for her. She stopped after taking two steps into the lobby, though.

Catalina stared at her surroundings – her mouth hanging in awe. The carpet throughout was a bright red with curtains to match on long gothic windows. All the wood throughout was deep and dark, shining as though every inch had been polished with linseed oil. A rich smell of fragrant flowers filled the lobby tall glass stands filled with fresh roses.

"You look like you're catching flies."

Catalina snapped her mouth shut. She pursed her lips into a thin line – her furrowed brows informing Matthew that he better contain his jovial nature if he wanted her to live up to her promise of behaving.

Her expression amused him and a flash of humor crossed his face.

"Welcome to the Windsor. May I help you?"

Startled, their heads bolted up to the attendant behind the front desk. He looked at them both expectantly – waiting for one of them to speak.

Matthew straightened to a serious stance. "Um, yes." He lifted the bag as though offering evidence. He "Yes, you may. We would like to rent a room for the evening." His tone exuded confidence.

"Two rooms." Catalina interjected.

"Yes. That's right." Matthew was thankful that the attendant didn't question them further. He simply placed two room keys on the counter. Matthew signed for the bill while another attendant came over to take them to their room.

Passing the dining room, Catalina wished they would have been led to rooms on the first floor. She was far too tired to climb the tall set of stairs leading to the second story of sleeping quarters.

"So… do we call it a night, or would you like to meet downstairs for dinner?" Matthew asked.

"For as beat as I am, I don't think I can afford to miss a meal." Catalina thought back to the earlier rumblings of her stomach. She pointed to the dining room. "Let's freshen up, then meet down there in an hour."

"Very well." Matthew remembered the time on the clock in the lobby. A quick bit of math and he nodded in agreement. "I'll ask the hotel to set a table for two at six o'clock."

"Agreed."

Catalina rushed out of her room. She hated being late to engagements – especially if it meant that her food was going to get cold. Unfortunately, she had entered the room to a welcoming bed. That required testing it for lumps. Of course, that meant laying down on it. Then the next thing she knew, the chime of a wall clock informed her that it was of the hour. Rushing about, changing out of her traveling dress, she pushed her hair back into a loose bun.

Still jabbing hair pins into her curls, she descended the stairs and ran right into a gentleman.

"Steady now, little lady."

Catalina hesitated at the sound of the familiar, unwelcomed voice.

The man with the jagged scar! What was he doing here?

She averted her eyes and mumbled an apology. "Excuse me, sir. I wasn't paying attention."

"Well, you should." The stranger's face held a menacing look. "You should thank me for saving your life as well. If I hadn't blocked your path, then you could have fallen down the stairs and broke your neck." The man reached out and ran a long index finger down her bare throat.

Catalina backed up a step, her hand flying to cover the scorching spot, blood pulsing beneath her trembling fingers. The taste of bile rose in her throat. "How dare you—"

She wanted to say more. Wanted to raise her hand and bring it down soundly across his face. In fact, she already had her hand raised to do the deed. However, an elderly woman ascended the stairs at that very moment.

"Good evening." A cautious glance at Catalina's hovering hand encouraged her to continue the ascent. She turned back around when she reached the top, eyeing them with suspicion of a lover's quarrel.

Catalina lowered her hand and glared at the stranger. She found renewed confidence in the presence of the older dame.

"I don't know who you are, sir." The words came out in a venomous whisper between clenched teeth. "Though, it matters not. What does matter is that I will undoubtedly have you arrested should you dare to accost me again."

The man flashed a broad, disturbing grin.

Catalina paid him no heed. She pushed past him – her head held high as though she were a queen who had just commanded a royal subject. However, her very core shook with fear.

There was something disturbingly familiar about that man.

She just couldn't place her finger on the reason why.

Catalina rounded the corner of the lobby, entered the dining room, and spotted Matthew sitting at a far corner table. A decorative porcelain vase filled with soft pink roses sat as a centerpiece. On either side of the flowers were small candles that illuminated their delicate petals – casting shadows on the wall beside Matthew's head.

It was odd since none of the other tables in the dining hall were bedecked in such fashion. In fact, none of them had any flowers at all, let alone roses.

The roses were the first thing that Matthew had thought to request from the hotel staff. He told them as he had told himself – it was the appropriate thing to do. A required gesture for a woman of class.

Certainly not because she carried the faint scent of roses since the first time he met her.

She sashayed towards him, a confident air about her as if she could command the moon and stars herself.

Matthew stood to offer her a chair. "You look lovely tonight."

"Thank you." She sat down with such fluidity, graceful as a dancer, yet her back remained rigid. . When she lifted a hand to pick up her napkin, her fingers trembled.

He cleared his throat. "Are you alright?"

Catalina positioned the napkin across her lap, smoothing a crease out of the soft cloth. "Oh, I'm fine.

Just a little tired." She spoke out of habit, but wondered if she should inform him of what had just occurred.

Hog spit.

Regardless of her reply, he could tell she was anything but fine. Still, he wouldn't press the matter and allow her space and ample opportunity to confide in him. "Well, if you're sure." Matthew motioned to the serving girl who immediately passed by a waiting station and picked up a silver pitcher. She poured sweet ice tea into the glasses that sat at each setting, and informed them that the house special was steak with potatoes, beans and tortillas.

They each nodded in eager consent, and thanked the girl before she left to fill their orders.

Catalina took another look at the flowers. A smile of appreciation touched her lips as she fingered the closest petal. "I didn't see these on any of the other tables. What's the special occasion?"

"The truth? I honestly don't know why I requested them. I just knew you liked roses, and thought you'd appreciate some after the difficulty you've had these past few days."

"That's so sweet of you. Thank you, Matthew. You're the first person to have shown any real concern for my feelings since—"

Since the accident.

Her voice had trailed off, but Matthew could fill in the blank. He had seen how everyone shunned the Santé family after word spread that Catalina had blood on her hands. It didn't seem to matter to people that she had acted in self-defense. They were all quick to assume that she was lying. Her family had gone from upstanding citizens, to "those foreigners" overnight.

Now he understood why she didn't want anything to do with her Mexican roots. Everyone considered her family acceptable under the notion that they were European – people of money. They would have been more than shunned if anyone thought they came from Mexico. With all the recent attacks throughout the Southwestern states, Catalina and her family could have easily faced a murderous mob.

He gave her a reassuring smile. "Don't worry about it. Soon there will be something bigger that comes along and catches everyone's attention. Then you'll be able to get on with your life as planned."

Catalina shook her head in disagreement. "I really don't think so." She tried to find the words to explain how she felt. "I just have this feeling that something isn't right. Almost like impending doom." She stared at her tea as though trying to focus her thoughts on what could possibly be wrong.

"It's probably nothing." Matthew tried to soothe her fears. "You're likely feeling exhausted from everything that has happened." Suddenly filled with sympathy for her situation, he reached over and patted the top of her hand.

She opened it and allowed his hand to latch onto hers. Lifting her eyes, slow and shy, she boldly searched his face. There was that feeling again. That pull to be with him, his very presence bringing a sense of calm. She would never have to worry about him having ulterior motives, or dishonorable secrets.

The serving girl appeared then with a tray holding their meal. Catalina sat back, her hand feeling like a lump of coal as it fell down into her lap.

Matthew nodded his thanks to the server before she took her leave. Grabbing hold of his knife, he cut a generous slice of the medium-well steak. He lifted the fork, but it hovered in front of his mouth.

Catalina sat silent, her head bowed in reverence. Her eyes were tightly shut, and her mouth silently moved in fervent prayer.

Matthew waited until her head rose again.

"Um... Do you *always* pray like that before you eat?" Uncomfortable and embarrassed, Matthew shifted in his seat. Maybe she wouldn't be offended if he asked her not to.

"Not always." Catalina said, cutting her steak into tiny pieces. "Sometimes I forget." She looked up with a sheepish grin as she thought of the biscuits she had scarfed down for breakfast. "It doesn't happen often – just when I'm especially distracted."

Matthew digested that bit of information along with the mouthful of steak he forced down. He wasn't too sure he cared for what he heard. He stammered to find the right words. "Well, I'm not trying to tell you what to do. It's just that I think I would appreciate it if you didn't do that when we're in public."

"Are you saying you don't want me to pray?"

"Well, kind of." Matthew placed his utensils down as he tried to explain it better. His hands moved as he spoke. "It's like this. Prayer is good and all – at the right time, in the right place. The right place is when you're at church. The wrong place is when you're out in public – like in a restaurant where everyone can see you."

Catalina's mouth hung open. After trying to piece together the right words to say – in which Matthew had resumed eating – she found her tongue.

"I'm sorry, but I'll have to respectfully disagree with you." She waited until she had Matthew's full attention. With renewed confidence, she made clear where she stood regarding her faith. "Devotion isn't only for Sundays. A relationship with God doesn't end once you leave the church. Would you choose not to talk to your own father because it wasn't Friday or Monday – or whatever other day you deemed sacred enough to do so?"

How would she react if she knew he never spoke to his father? But that particular topic was best left for another time. When it wasn't so raw and painful. "I get what you're saying. I really do." Matthew conceded. Why ruin a nice dinner over talk of God? It wasn't like he didn't believe himself. "And I agree that you *should* be able to pray wherever you want. After all, it's your faith. However, I just think it would make everyone more comfortable if you didn't do it so visibly."

Besides, I don't think He cares much about what we're really going through.

Matthew didn't voice why he didn't believe God cared. If God really cared, then He would've given Matthew a better father – one who wouldn't have made his childhood so difficult. One who would have actually wanted him, and stuck around when it mattered most. No, he couldn't tell her that.

He couldn't admit that to anyone.

Matthew looked up to find Catalina's watchful eyes studying him. He shifted uncomfortably. Concentrating on his food, he cut another thick chunk of steak. "This needs a little *pico de gallo*." He stuffed the meat into a tortilla with a few spoons of beans and fried potatoes.

Did she dare argue the importance of prayer, regardless of the place or occasion?

Death and life are in the power of the tongue…

Catalina wasn't entirely sure which proverb had just come to mind. She did believe in the wisdom of it, though. She had better pick her battles wisely.

"What is *pico de gallo*?" she asked, intrigued by the way the words felt on her tongue.

"You don't know what it is?" He sputtered while forcing the remainder of his food past his throat. The lump left behind forced him to take a swig of his tea Catalina raised the napkin and dabbed at the corner of her mouth in an attempt to hide a smile. "No. I've never heard of anything so strange."

"Well, it's Spanish," Matthew began.

"I gathered that." Catalina wasn't prone to interrupting people when they were speaking, but she had always been taught that an educated woman shouldn't allow herself to be taken as a fool just for a man's sake. "Along with Italian lessons, my parents insisted that I learn some Spanish when I was younger. I may be a little rusty after so many years of only speaking English. However, I think I may still be able to translate a word or two."

Matthew laid his utensils down and sat back in his chair. He folded his arms across his chest as a slow, challenging look painted his face. "Go on then. I'm listening."

Catalina placed her napkin back in her lap and folded her hands in front of her. She rested her chin in her hands as she thought about what each individual word meant.

"Let's see. *Gallo* means rooster. That I know."

A broad smile stretched across Matthew's face. Amusement danced in his eyes.

"*Pico* literally means a beak or bill." Catalina looked quizzically at Matthew. It was obvious that he was silently laughing at her. "Oh, come now. I know you don't really want a rooster beak to go with our meal."

A deep, throaty laugh escaped and he pounded a fist against the table.

"Shhh... Hush now." Catalina motioned for him to quiet as she spied other diners glaring at them. She swatted at him with her napkin in a playful manner. It only brought his jolly roar down to a rumbling chuckle.

"I'm sorry." He used the back of his hand to wipe away a tear. "I just had a vision of a rooster pecking at our food while we were trying to eat."

Now it was Catalina's turn to find the humor in the situation.

She drew her lips together in a tight smile. Soon she was hiding her face in her hands – silently laughing into them. She finally looked up only to see Matthew shaking a finger at her.

"See, these are the kinds of things I'm thankful for."

It took a moment for the laughter to completely die down. Then it only took a second longer before Catalina realized this was her window of opportunity.

"If that's true, then you should offer up a prayer of thanksgiving. Don't you think so?" Catalina's eyes drew into small slits as they challenged him.

Matthew's face slowly clouded over and grew serious. He didn't like being cornered into making decisions about things he'd rather leave alone.

"I thought that part of the conversation was over." He drank some more tea to clear his throat. "In fact, I know we're finished discussing the matter."

He said it so resolutely. It appeared that she wouldn't be able to change his mind, regardless of what she said.

Catalina swallowed the lump that had formed in her throat. The topic of their argument made it all too clear that Matthew wasn't a believer. The fact that it bothered her as much as it did made her aware of one very undeniable fact.

She cared for him.

Tears gathered behind her thick lashes. She abruptly stood and tossed her napkin on the table as one threatened to spill out.

"That is really too bad."

Matthew stared at her in confusion. "What are you talking about?"

Unable to answer, she merely waved him off as she headed to her room.

"Hey, wait a minute." Matthew stood, with every intention of following her. One look around the dining hall told him just how much attention they had drawn to themselves. He sat back down in his seat – grumbling under his breath about *wishy washy* women.

Matthew looked back to where Catalina had stalked off.

Now what in the world has gotten into her?

Chapter Eight

The plush blankets and down pillows did little to ease Catalina's spirit. She draped across the four poster canopy bed, an arm dangling off the edge of one side.

How could she have fallen for yet another man who didn't share the same faith? Why did she keep doing this?

And what business did she have falling in love anyway?

A wearisome sigh escaped her lips. This exact kind of foolishness was the cause of her life's upheaval to begin with. She wasn't about to allow yet another man worm his way into her heart – no matter how handsome or funny he was.

No matter how charming he is.

The roses he had ordered for the table were such a sweet gesture. The only way he would have known that roses were her favorite flowers is if he had picked up on the fragrance she wore.

At least he thought about her. Too bad it could only ever be a dream.

Why?

Catalina sat up. Why couldn't they be together?

Truth be told, a part of her didn't think she deserved to be with anyone. She had taken away a man's life – even if by accident. She couldn't trust her own judgment. And if she couldn't trust herself, then she certainly couldn't trust him.

Not really.

Then trust me.

The small, still voice seemed so reassuring, but should she heed it or follow the path being laid before her? How could she be sure which was the right one?

She groaned and rubbed her face as if she could invigorate herself by doing so. She didn't want to think about the right path, or men or even the roses she had left behind on the table.

They could have been a very useful keepsake.

"Oh, well." Catalina waved that thought off, then gathered her dressing gown and made her way to the wash closet. Adjusting the handles until steam began to fill the room, she drew back the curtain. A small splash of oil and the bath looked inviting enough to never leave. She dipped her toes into the warm water, and virtually sank like stone into the large porcelain tub.

Catalina's aches slowly began to ease, and she grew drowsy from the hot water that engulfed her. As her lids grew heavy, her final thoughts once again revolved around a pair of blue eyes the color and depth of the ocean.

Matthew didn't like to see good food go to waste. And he also wasn't one to go chasing after a woman who would get her feathers all ruffled just because he didn't see much need for prayer. Although he sure as shootin' wanted to find her and make amends. He ran the highlights of their conversation in his mind, realizing that Catalina's mood changed the moment their spiritual views differed.

If something so silly was going to set her off, then he'd rather let her have her pout and try to start fresh in the morning.

Matthew polished off the rest of his ice tea, and tossed a couple of bills onto the table. Making his way to his room, he almost ran into another gentleman.

"Pardon me."

The man simply nodded and continued on his way – leaving Matthew just a little baffled.

That guy looks strangely familiar.

It must have been an hour or longer since Catalina had climbed into the tub. She couldn't be too sure of the time, but the water had turned frigid.

Texas nights in July were colder than she would have expected.

Standing, she drew back the curtain and hurried to grab a towel. It was only after she had stepped out of the tub and pulled the drain that she gave any real attention to the darkened bedroom, only lit by the soft glow of the bathroom. How could she have stayed in the tub so long?

It still wasn't enough light for her. The dark was the one thing she didn't care for. She could deal with anything else.

Well, almost anything else.

She definitely couldn't deal with the man from the ferry. It had been the first time that she had been afraid to be on a boat.

A knock at the door forced Catalina into her dressing gown.

"Who is it?"

Catalina clucked her tongue like a mama hen as she rolled her eyes. Only one person would knock on her door at this hour.

What audacity of Matthew to pay her a visit after sundown! And to stand at her door without answering? She shook her head at his surprising lack of social skills.

Catalina walked over to the closed door, but refused to open it at such a late hour.

"Matthew, I'm really quite exhausted and have just finished getting ready for bed. Let's talk in the morning, please."

Silence, and then the knob jiggled, the lock jerking as if someone were trying to unlock it from the outside.

Matthew works for the law. He wouldn't try to break into my room.

Catalina scanned the room, her gaze snagging on the curvy leather armchair in the far corner of the room. She could use it to bar the door! Racing over, she gave it a strong tug, but only managed to move it an inch from its original spot.

Useless piece of...

Frantic, she pressed her face against the cool glass, peering down at the quiet street below, her heart beating in her throat. Could she jump out the window to get help? No. She would never make the trip down without breaking a leg – or worse.

Should she scream? Would anyone even be able to hear her behind the closed door?

She sprinted back into the bathroom and turned on the faucet in the tub. Then she tugged the curtains closed and dashed back out – leaving the door partially cracked behind her.

Just as she pressed herself against the cold, hard floor, she heard the lock snap.

Click.

One swift push and Catalina slid under the bed, the thick dust tickling her nose. She opened her mouth – trying to draw in soft, even breaths, but that didn't calm her nerves. Her entire body quivered with such fear that she could feel the small beads of sweat forming above her brow. Worse was the sudden sensation of having to see to womanly needs, her abdomen cramping in urgency.

The door creaked, and light from the hallway spilled in. The prowler's boots were black and brown, a mix between leather and something scaly. There was also a gold insignia on one that looked like a snake with a sword through it.

The intruder took his time, moving with deft ease like someone practiced in the ways of unlawful entry. His smooth, slow glide along the wood floors hardly made any noise at all.

What if she had been asleep? She would have never heard him.

He paused only a few feet in front of her hiding place.

Please don't look under the bed!

She was out of escape routes.

And oxygen! She couldn't hold her breath any longer.

The intruder stepped toward the bathroom.

Thank You, Lord! Catalina let out her pent up breath, drawing in a slow, deep one to ease the dizziness that cloaked her mind. Staying hidden under the bed, she slid to the far corner of the room, and added distance between herself and this new terror.

The cool floor did little to ease the heat blanketing her limbs. She slithered out from under the bed just as the man disappeared into the bathroom. Crouching, she clung onto the mattress and commanded her feet to move.

Run...

RUN, YOU FOOLISH GIRL!

And she did. She bounded two steps forward before the floor beneath her creaked in protest, betraying her whereabouts.

Catalina's hand squeezed the door handle when one heavy arm landed around her waist, the other latched around her throat.

He jerked her back, but she held tight to the handle and yanked the door open.

The light from the hallway poured into the room, and she reached out to it for salvation.

The man dragged her further into the dark room, her struggles no match for his brute power.

Fear coursed through her veins. She screamed, but his beefy hand muffled the sound, his grip tightening until the world faded to black. She mashed her bare heel into his boot.

"You'll pay for that!" Her attacker stepped back, but didn't release his hold.

Her breathing slowed into shallow gasps. Time suspended. Her only priority was to breathe.

Most of her energy gone, she thought to do the first thing that came to mind before she lost all consciousness.

She relaxed her limbs, making herself limp as a beaten ragdoll.

The man's hold loosened slightly. Not enough to run away, but plenty to do as planned. Now if only her plan worked!

In one smooth motion, she pressed her back against his chest – her hands reaching up and blocking the space between his forearm and her neck.

The man stiffened and cursed, fumbled with position.

But it was too late.

Catalina bit down on the man's arm, intent on drawing blood, gritting past the vile mixture of dirt and sweat.

Her assailant cursed again, encasing a fistful of her hair and yanking until surely skin separated from skull.

She screamed, a sound loud enough to curdle her own blood. Was that really her?

Catalina's cry of pain turned into a call for help and there was a commotion somewhere out in the hall of doors opening, and hotel guests asking what was going on. The sound of footsteps followed, and Matthew bound through the door.

Doors. Murmurs, raised and soft. Footsteps pounded the floor.

Was that Matthew's voice?

She couldn't open her eyes, the blinding pain threatening to explode.

The assailant jerked her head back then slammed it, her scalp connecting wood.

Then, blessed relief. Released by her captor, she staggered, slumped to the floor, warmth trickling down her face.

Glass shattered.

She forced her eyelids open, only slits, but wide enough to see Matthew hovering over her before everything faded away.

Chapter Nine

Something soft and fuzzy rubbed against Catalina's cheek. She tried opening her eyes to see what it was, but her lids felt heavy. Then she had the strange sensation of floating through air. Nausea gripped her stomach, and the taste of acid rose like a lump in her throat. She swallowed hard against it as she was slowly lowered back down, and lay on the cool floor.

Groaning, she made an attempt to push herself up. Her body trembled in protest, though. She fell back into the soft fuzz and surrendered to the darkness.

"Come on, honey. Open your eyes."

Matthew lightly stroked Catalina's cheek in an attempt to awaken her. He ignored the crowd of hotel guests that had stepped out of their rooms to investigate the commotion. He couldn't blame them. Her shrill scream had summoned him as well. The last thing he expected was to see Catalina wrestling a man twice her size. Then to see where she had hit her head? It was enough to keep from tearing through the hotel, searching for the rogue who had attacked her.

Why had he been in her room anyway? Did she know him? Was he just some common thief, and she an unfortunate target?

Or was the incident connected to something bigger?

So many questions rolled around in his head like a shady set of dice that all landed back at the same point of origin…

Catalina.

Another pitiful groan sounded and he tried to sit her up again. He put some distance between them this time – aware of the fact that his current form of dress, or lack thereof, was certainly against protocol in the presence of decent women.

The last thing he wanted was for anyone to accuse either of them of committing some scandalous act of impropriety.

"What's going on here?" The hotel manager pushed through the crowd, demanding an explanation.

"That man hurt that girl."

An elderly gent with an ounce of bravado pointed a shaky finger at Matthew. A crinkly, stern-looking woman – undoubtedly his wife – stood beside him, nodding her head enthusiastically.

Matthew felt his neck turn warm as the temperature of his anger rose.

"I most certainly did not!"

His voice rumbled and scared the crowd as each syllable escalated like thunder.

"I came running out here just in time to see some maniac jump out of her window." Matthew shook his head in disbelief. He still couldn't believe who would be crazy enough to pull such a stunt. If the guy wasn't in a crumpled heap outside, then he must have suffered a broken leg at the very least. And, boy, he'd sure like to get down there and see. Maybe he could catch the guy! "Please. Can you at least send for a doctor?"

The last comment was directed at the manager, who then turned to one of the attendants to do just that.

The young man scampered off and bounded down the stairs in twos. Meanwhile, the manager tried to take hold of the situation.

"Alright. Alright. Everyone just take a step back, and give the girl a chance to breathe." He crouched opposite from Matthew and spoke lowly. "You sure you didn't have a hand in this, Mister?"

Matthew could feel his temperature rising again. Afraid of grabbing hold of the man and delivering a good shaking, he squeezed his eyes shut and commanded himself to calm down. Instead, his jaws clenched tighter and the sound of grinding teeth echoed in his own head.

"Ouch." Catalina came to and struggled to sit up. "I feel like I just rammed my head against a brick."

"Close enough." The image of her head clashing against the bedpost would haunt him for a long time. He pushed the horrible reminder and braced an arm around Catalina's back to help her stand. "Take your time now. No need to rush… Just slow and steady like."

Catalina stood and could feel the world tilt again. She leaned into Matthew and placed her hand flat against his chest, surprised at the curly patch of dark hair.

"Oh, I'm terribly sorry." Her words sounded rehearsed – as if she were simply saying that which propriety dictated. She really wasn't sorry at all, if her thundering pulse was any indication. However, the elation was fleeting as her head began to throb.

"Um, that's alright. I mean to say that…" Matthew stumbled over the words as he gently removed her hand and placed it in the crook of his arm, offering support. "I was getting ready to turn in for the night when I heard you scream. Naturally, there wasn't much time to fumble with a button-up shirt."

"Naturally."

He had to give her credit. She looked pretty worse for the wear, but was trying her hardest to downplay the pain.

Matthew nodded at the hotel manager. Realizing his assistance was no longer needed, the man took a step back. "Alright, everyone. I think we've had enough excitement for one night. You can all head back to your rooms now."

An immediate ruckus ensued. Guests questioned whether they were safe in such a hotel. One highfalutin woman demanded a refund for the fright she had to endure. The manager's cheeks rounded with red blotches as he blustered over the idea of returning money.

"George! What's going on out there?" An aged voice sounded from behind one of the doors, saving the poor man.

"There's a half-naked woman out here, Martha!" A rickety man called out to his wife while pointing at Catalina.

What? Who? Her? Catalina glanced down, horrified that she only wore a nightgown. Fire flamed her cheeks and her hands flew to her nightgown.

"Well, get in here right now and you can see a whole lot more than that!"

The poor man shook his head sadly. "I know, I know." He mumbled under his breath. "Heaven, help me. I know."

Laughter erupted, and the crowd dispersed.

"Come on." Matthew tried to pull Catalina towards his room. It seemed like she was glued to the floor, though. He followed her line of sight to a well-dressed gent.

Anger glittered from her eyes.

"You!" Seething, Catalina pointed to the man that stood at the other end of the hall. "You're responsible for this."

Several individuals – including the hotel manager – paused when she spoke. The stranger looked around at everyone with surprise registered on his face. "I beg your pardon, Miss. I don't have the slightest idea what you're talking about."

"It was you." Catalina took a step forward, but Matthew held onto her. She tried to tug her arm away from him – the movement causing her head to throb harder. She brought her hand up to her head and spoke slowly.

"I'm telling you it was him. He was behind all of this."

A clouded look passed over Matthew's face. He continued to hold onto Catalina, but addressed the stranger. "What's she talking about, Mister? Who are you?"

"No one that has to answer to the likes of you." The man hooked his thumbs in the side of his pant pockets and rocked on his heels. A cocky grin challenged Matthew to fight.

Matthew pushed Catalina behind him and took a step forward. His stance was wide as he balled his fists. "My name is Deputy Martin, and I say you'll answer me or enjoy the hard bed of a cold cell tonight."

A voice called up from the staircase. "I think you might be speaking out of turn, Son." A long, wiry man wearing a faded pair of blue jeans and matching button-down shirt winded his way up the stairs. "Name's

Durbin. That's *Sheriff* John Durbin, so I'll handle things from here."

Matthew sized him up quickly.

A bushy auburn mustache hung on either side of his crooked jaw like a horseshoe. He wore a tall Stetson that seemed just a little too nice for the rest of his outfit. It was obvious just by his walk that the man wasn't someone to mess around with. If the mean glint in his eye didn't convince a person that he meant business, then the pistol that hung off his hip and the badge that read "Sheriff" would most likely do the job.

Matthew conceded to the man with a simple nod. He wouldn't want anyone superseding his say had it been his jurisdiction.

"A hotel attendant came running out to the square a few minutes ago. He made an awful ruckus, yelling for a doctor. So what happened and who was involved?"

Catalina hesitantly raised a hand. "I was, sir."

"And I was not." The stranger volunteered the information before further guilt could be placed on him.

"This man has been following me since Mississippi!" Catalina glared at the man with accusing eyes.

Sheriff Durbin was quick to prevent a possible argument. "Hold up now, folks." He commanded silence with a slight gesture of his raised hands. He eyed the few stragglers that still meandered around the hotel corridor. "Did anyone else see anything, or have anything to contribute to these two here?" The sheriff motioned between the stranger and Catalina.

A few individuals eagerly shook their heads. Others simply looked away.

"Alright now. Y'all be on your way." The sheriff looked between the two parties. "I'll speak with each of you privately."

"But not until after I've examined the girl." A spry, elderly gent appeared at the top of the stairs. Wide rim spectacles were outlined by thin, gray windblown hair. He briskly walked towards them as though on a mission.

Catalina suddenly realized how they must look, both only half-dressed and standing close enough to touch.

"Evening, Doc."

"Hello, John. Don't forget what I told you yesterday. Come by the house before you ride out west."

"Will do," Sheriff Durbin answered, his gaze focused on the doctor as the man guided Catalina into a room before transferring back to the stranger again. "So what's your name, Mister?"

"Thomas Delany of Mississippi."

"And why are you following us?" Matthew stepped forward – his arms crossed in front of his bare chest. He stood beside the sheriff, hopeful that the snarl of his upper lip looked menacing enough to scare the man into being truthful. He stared at the man's jagged scar. "I remember you now. You were that fella' on the ferry in Mississippi."

"Indeed I was." Mr. Delany nodded his head in confirmation. "I'm on my way to Silver City in New Mexico. I have a claim there that I like to check on every now and then."

Sherriff Durbin picked back up on the interrogation. "And where were you in this last little while?"

A wicked smile touched Mr. Delany's face. "Tasting the delights of Abilene. I believe her name was Beth." The man sucked the tips of his fingers as though he had just finished eating fried chicken.

Matthew's stomach churned.

"Well, I'll be checking out your story." The sheriff ignored the man's crude gesture. "So, don't leave town."

Mr. Delany bowed forward in a flashy show. "As you wish, Sheriff." He took a few steps back and hovered near the top of the stairs.

Matthew ignored him and turned towards Catalina when the sheriff stopped him.

"And what's your story, Son? You seem to be a little underdressed." He eyed Matthew in a way that declared the ability to sniff out the whitest of lies.

Matthew wasn't about to turn into the town crier.

"I'm Deputy Martin of Mecklenburg County, North Carolina. I've been hired to escort Ms. Santé to some family she has along the Arizona border." He continued to stand in the same stance. "And there wasn't any time to grab a shirt when I heard Ms. Santé scream."

Sheriff Durbin looked at Matthew for a long minute, but thankfully failed to ask more detailed questions – such as just which side of the border Catalina's family was located.

"And do you have any ideas as to who would want to harm Ms. Santé?"

Matthew wanted to pin the incident on any number of the Monroe clan, but had no proof that it had been one of them – not to mention the further attention it would bring if the locals found out that Catalina stood accused of homicide.

Besides, all of the decent folks in Charlotte had been fast asleep when they left town.

Matthew shook his head. "Not off the top of my head."

Mr. Delany cleared his throat in an obnoxious attempt to be heard. "I wouldn't be surprised one bit if some *bandito* saw that pretty little Miss, and thought to just snatch her right up."

Matthew squinted at the over-opinionated man and sized him up.

If it were just the two of us alone, I bet I could—

"I wouldn't be surprised if you're right." Sheriff Durbin interrupted Matthew's thoughts with an unfortunate dose of reality. "We've been having a lot of trouble with those sorts ever since Villa made his way through. Now every Mexi-*can* thinks he can take whatever he sees – some sort of misconception that this was their land first, so everything on it is theirs, too."

"Well, there you have it – the reason we've got our troops all along the frontier." Mr. Delany sucked on his teeth and rocked back on his heels. Then he drove home his point. "Ain't just them Krauts we've got to worry about after all."

Matthew shoved his fists in his pockets to keep from throwing one in the man's face. "You gentlemen will have to excuse me. It's been a long night and I'd like to get some rest – not to mention a shirt." He ignored Mr. Delany, but nodded his goodnight to the sheriff.

"I'll be questioning the hotel manager next. I'll send him up after I do so he can speak with Ms. Santé about securing a new room."

"No need." Matthew spoke in a manner that left no room for argument. "Ms. Santé is my charge, and I won't allow another incident like this one to occur. So I'll be keeping watch over her for the rest of the evening."

One man hiked a brow a mile high. The other smirked. He'd love to wipe that evil grin clean away. Instead, he nodded a brief "goodnight" to both, though he couldn't see anything good about it.

Chapter Ten

"Well, it's no surprise you have a headache. You have quite a goose egg on your head." The doctor mixed some concoction. "Drink this. You'll feel better in the morning."

Catalina sat up higher on the mountain of pillows that the physician had made for her. She eagerly reached out for the homemade brew.

"Thank you very much." She took a sip from the cup and then forced down the bitter drink.

His crinkly face smiled expectantly.

Did he really expect praise for his medicine? Telling him it tasted good would be a lie. She opted for diplomacy instead.

"You've been too kind – coming out here so late at night." She tried to take another sip from the cup, hiding another grimace as the liquid reached her lips. "How much do I owe you for the visit?"

"You just worry about resting." The doctor patted her hand, and then picked up his bag to leave. "I'll discuss my fee with your husband."

Her husband? Matthew? She blushed at the thought of how he had held her in the hall. It was only natural that the doctor would wrongly assume the nature of their relationship.

She stared down at the quilt that covered her, and lightly began tracing the stitches of the intricate star pattern. How could she possibly explain her awkward situation? She squeezed her eyes and prayed for the right words.

"Well, he isn't actually my—"

Heavy boots pounded the old pine floors.

Catalina's eyes flickered open.

Matthew! The sight of him confidently walking into the room made her mouth snap shut.

Matthew stood at the foot of the bed, weighing the situation. The evening's earlier attack reminded him of countless moments from his past, with the worst one being a raid on some of Villa's men a couple of years earlier. That was why he had left the territory. The land was wild and dangerous, and there was no way of knowing if anyone would come around looking to claim their pound of flesh in exchange for the ones he took. Was he about to be dragged back into the unknown?

For her?

He looked at Catalina, their eyes connecting momentarily. Then his slowly drifted downward to her exposed cotton negligee. Something raw and feral flashed in Matthew's eyes. Catalina dipped her head with embarrassment, nervously tugging the quilt closer to her chin.

"Uh…" Matthew shook his head and ran a hand through his own tangled hair as if that could dispel the sight of Catalina lying in his bed – her innocent doe eyes and tousled curls signifying the nearing start of a new day. He had no business thinking such ungentlemanly thoughts.

Distraction. He needed a distraction. He forced his gaze away from the bed. He caught sight of his shirt draped across the back of the settee, and made his way over to the faded plaid fabric. Slipping the shirt on, he worked the buttons before addressing the doctor.

"So what's the prognosis?"

"Well, she has a nasty bump on her head that needed a couple of stitches. There's some bruising, too."

How could a man harm a woman? The very thought made him mad enough to consider grabbing a pistol and searching the streets for the lowlife who could do something as underhanded as attack a helpless woman in her own room. At night.

While under *his* protection.

Matthew's jaw flexed and the sound of his clenching teeth filled the room.

"Oh, don't worry. She'll live." The doctor waved away any real concern and winked. "I gave her a little something that will make her sleep like a baby."

Matthew raised a suspicious brow. He looked over at Catalina who continued to sip from a mug – a sheepish grin suggesting what he already suspected was the prescribed treatment.

Laudanum.

Matthew contained a frown at the thought of Catalina downing the substance. The law had restricted the use of the addictive tincture just a few years earlier. However, it wasn't actually illegal. And many doctors still relied on it to cure everything from excruciating pain to simple coughs.

Catalina drained the cup and slowly placed it down on a small nightstand. Then she pulled the covers under her chin and smiled up at him. A small giggle escaped her lips, which she tried to cover with her delicate fingers.

Matthew bit back a smile and motioned for the doctor to follow. "Let's step outside and finish talking."

The doctor bid Catalina a good evening, but she responded with a lazy wave

With his hand twisting the doorknob, Matthew glanced back into the room.

Catalina had already slipped away into some tranquil place of dreams.

What would it be like to…?

It wasn't the daylight pouring into the room that caused Catalina to stir, but the soft knock at her door.

Lifting her tired body made her feel otherworld. She ached all over like a whipped cur, her head heavy and stiff as she raised it.

As though in a dreamy haze, she floated to the door.

And opened it to a nightmare.

"No. It isn't possible." She shook her head as though it could make Benjamin's image disappear. "I saw you. You're dead."

Benjamin smiled down at her – one of those sweet smiles she remembered from their first meeting. Catalina's heart skipped a beat as she tried to make amends.

"I'm so sorry for what I did. I never meant for it to happen." Her throat and eyes began to burn as she held back tears. "Do you forgive me?"

Benjamin simply stood there, looking down at her with a smile so strange that it sent a shiver down her spine. The hair on the back of her neck stood on end, and she began to shake with fear.

"Well, don't just stand there." She commanded him to break his silence. "Say something!"

Benjamin's soft smile turned sinister. "I only came to finish the job."

Without warning, his thick hands shot out and circled her throat.

She chirped a protest, short and shrill, cut off by his tightened pressure. Then she gasped for air.

"Catalina." He called out her name as he shook her. "Come on, girl."

She fought against the fiend of her nightmare. Her small hands reached out to claw, but fell short of their target.

He called out to her again. "Wake up, Catalina!"

The fog quickly dissipated, and Catalina shook off the groggy nightmare. She opened her eyes to find Matthew staring down at her.

The sunlight streamed into the room, framing Matthew in such a way that made him seem like an angel come to rescue her.

She must have made for a frightful sight. Raising a trembling hand, she smoothed down wild hair that had worked its way out of her braid.

"You must have been having some dream."

He sank onto the bed beside her – his strong hands warming her shoulders as he helped her sit up. The covers slipped away, leaving her light cotton nightgown exposed.

Catalina tugged the cover back up to her chin as Matthew stood and stepped away from the bed.

She did her best to ignore the awkward moment. The last thing she wanted to admit to anyone – especially him – was the truth about whom she had been dreaming about. What if he thought she still had feelings for an old beau?

"It was a rough night." She managed a small smile even though she still felt like a bundle of jittery nerves.

"Well, that's putting it mildly." His voice went soft with concern.

"You have no idea." Catalina closed her eyes and laid her head back. All she wanted to do was forget that it had ever happened. "I hope I never experience anything like that ever again."

"That's why I barged in here like that. I heard you screaming again." He ran a hand through his hair. Her sharp trills had given him a start that he still couldn't shake off. "I thought someone had managed to slip by me, or something."

"Slip by you?" Catalina studied him for a moment, the weight of his words sinking in. "Did you spend the entire night in the hallway?"

Heat crept up Matthew's neck. He tried to rub away the embarrassment.

"I had to. I made a personal vow to protect people when I started working for the law." He shifted a bit as though uncomfortable to continue. "And it would have sent tongues a-wagging if we had spent last night together."

A raised eyebrow confirmed that his last statement had come out all wrong.

"I didn't mean to put it quite like that." He looked for the right words to say. "Um…"

"You don't have to explain." She rushed in to save him. "I understand."

Catalina glanced behind him and noticed the door wide open.

She looked down before speaking.

"I suppose you were doing what any good deputy would have done." Sadness filled her eyes as she spoke. "At least, I hope that's true. You've been one of the few people I've ever known who actually seems concerned for my welfare."

Matthew didn't know where the thought came from, but was reminded of a scripture he had read long ago. He didn't believe in the God much, but he had been interested in one part of the Bible.

"Well, it's like the Good Book says." Matthew paused for a moment as he recalled the exact words. "'Whoever forces you to go one mile, go with him two.'"

Catalina beamed up at him. "You know Scripture!"

"Not really."

Her smile deflated just a little, but it was best she knew the truth.

"I've only ever read the book of Matthew." Reluctant and awkward, he shrugged. "I thought it was a good idea since I had the same name, but I'll be honest... I don't even remember which verse that is."

Catalina closed her eyes and thought for a moment.

"You know, the book of Matthew is one of my favorites, but I'll be honest, too. I don't remember the Scripture at all." She pointed at her bag on the floor. "I believe my Bible is in there. Could you check for me, please?"

Matthew fished around in the bag and pulled out the small Bible – the leather cover only slightly worn.

He held it out to her, but she shook her head.

"Would you mind finding it while I get ready?"

The look on his face suggested that he wasn't very keen about the idea. Still, he agreed to the simple task and turned to leave.

"Wait!"

Matthew paused and looked back at her. She bit her lip. How would he react to her next request? "Will you let me do one thing before you go?"

Matthew looked at her questionably, but agreed and pulled the chair close to the bed.

Please, Father. Give me the right words to say.

She placed her small hand into his larger one, ignoring the warmth and zing of pleasure of his touch. She closed her eyes and bowed her head. He followed suit as she began to pray.

Matthew only had a slight idea what she was referring to as she prayed about no longer being thirsty. Then she asked God to shine a light into their open hearts.

He listened to the soft murmur of an "Amen," but failed to say the same. He could only sit there, stunned. The only other person who had ever prayed over him was his mother when he was a small child.

Matthew swallowed the thick feeling lumping in his throat. An overpowering emotion stuck in his chest. He tried to shake it off, but there was no denying it.

This was a lot more than simply being attracted to a pretty face.

He drew in a long, shaky breath as he stood. There was something he wanted – no, needed – to say.

He opened his mouth to speak – the words hanging on the tip of his tongue, but the proclamation died. Instead of confessing how he felt, he simply raised the Bible.

He nodded, meeting her challenge, then strode away – leaving Catalina to stare after him in utter confusion.

She had felt the charge in the air. Hadn't she?

She brushed it off.

Once he shut the door, Catalina took a moment to absorb the peaceful silence.

She had intended to pray for Matthew. Instead, she had asked God to open both their hearts.

As if a still, small voice had commanded her, Catalina knew she needed to cast aside her uncertainty.

It was time she searched her own doubting heart, and accepted what was there.

Chapter Eleven

The Bible sat open beside Matthew's cup of coffee like a gateway to another world. From the moment he had picked it up, the words had burned into him like an engraving on delicate jewelry.

"Father, forgive them, for they know not what they do."

How could anyone be kind to those who had shown him such cruelty?

The very thought that someone could be so willing to sacrifice himself so that others could have hope and salvation unraveled Matthew's mind. A thirst to learn more kept him flipping pages.

"That's some mighty fine reading right there."

Matthew nearly jumped out of his seat. He had been so lost in the message that he hadn't heard anyone approach him.

"Morning, Sheriff." Matthew rose to shake the man's hand. "A few days away from the boys back home and it looks like I'm losing my touch. No one's ever been able to catch me off guard like that." He motioned for Sheriff Durbin to take the seat in front of him.

"Well, I've been snaking around for a bit." The sheriff sat in the chair while signaling a serving girl. It was the same one who had given Matthew a saucy wink right after Catalina stormed off the night before. She kept her head down this time, and he could only assume it was because of the reprimand he had given her.

"A cup of mud, please."

She cautiously glanced over at Matthew's cup to check if it needed to be refilled. Seeing that it did not, she scurried off without as much as a word.

Thankfully, Sheriff Durbin either didn't notice or care to acknowledge the girl's cold nature. The last thing Matthew needed was for anyone to question his character. A misunderstanding with local law enforcement would just complicate things.

"I've been thinking about last night." Sheriff Durbin said.

Matthew closed the Bible and gave the sheriff his full attention.

The man sat there examining his nails as though they needed a good cleaning.

Matthew could feel the hair on the back of his neck stand. Something told him that he wasn't going to enjoy this conversation very much.

"What about last night?"

The seasoned sheriff focused on Matthew, his eyes sharp with purpose. "I've been thinking that maybe this attack wasn't some coincidence."

"What do you mean?"

"You didn't really think I'd let an incident like last night occur without further investigation, did you?" Sheriff Durbin spoke directly. "I checked you out – both of y'all, that is. I know all about the accident in Carolina."

Matthew opened his mouth and clapped it shut again. He couldn't very well lie. At the same time he wasn't sure if admitting the truth would cause further problems.

He was still forming a response when Catalina sulked into the room.

Why was the sheriff sitting at the same table as Matthew? Had he uncovered news about her attacker?

"Good morning, gentlemen." Both men stood as she took a seat.

"Good morning, Ms. Santé."

Catalina reached for her napkin. Wait! The sheriff had called her by her last name! Her hand hovered over the neatly folded cloth. How had he learned who she was? Matthew had registered the rooms under his name. Surely he hadn't said anything.

Then again, maybe he had. After all, Matthew was a deputy, too.

Catalina lifted the napkin and placed it on her lap, spearing Matthew with a lifted brow.

He shook his head in the negative.

Catalina looked pointedly at the sheriff.

"I don't recall giving you my name, Sheriff… Durbin?"

The sheriff's head bobbled. "Yes, that is correct. My last name is Durbin – first name is John." He paused as the serving girl returned with his coffee. She offered a small apology in how long it took to deliver – explaining that it had to brew first.

"So now we know who you are," Matthew continued once the girl had left again. "However, that doesn't quite explain how you know of us – although I can imagine how you got the information."

"And how do you believe I came about it?"

As if Matthew didn't know Sheriff Durbin was asking leading questions, trying to draw information out of them. "How about you tell me? If you're right, then I'll let you know."

"Fair enough," the sheriff began. "The first thing that caught my attention was that you registered for two rooms."

"That's not a crime." Matthew sat back and crossed his arms in front of his chest.

"No. It's not a crime – just strange." The sheriff took a gulp of his coffee before continuing. "Kind of telling too. If y'all were married or siblings, then you would have shared a room."

Catalina piped up. "Not necessarily. Why should a woman have to share a room with her brother?"

"She doesn't have to," Sheriff Durbin smiled. "But he ain't your brother."

"And how do you know he isn't?"

"Darling, I have sisters of my own." The sheriff's grin broadened. "And I never looked at any of them the way he looked at you last night."

Matthew choked and nearly spat out his drink. He glanced over at Catalina. A deep rose color crept along her cheeks. She refused to look at him – instead focusing on the plate in front of her.

Was she embarrassed about being put on the spot, or just about the topic of conversation?

Matthew bolted out of his seat, throwing his napkin on the table. "What are you getting on about, friend?"

Sheriff Durbin lazily motioned for him to sit back down.

He complied.

"Now don't get your dander up, working yourself into a tizzy over nothing. Let's just skip to the meat and potatoes."

"Please do," Catalina pleaded. "So we can get on to the real meat and potatoes. Some of us haven't had the pleasure of breakfast just yet."

"My apologies, ma'am. Allow me to stir up a server for you."

"No, don't." The urgency of the statement made Catalina's voice sound almost too sharp. She lowered her voice again. "I don't think I much care for anyone listening in on our conversation."

Matthew agreed. "How about you just finish telling us what you were fixin' to say?"

Sheriff Durbin nodded empathetically. "Fair enough. After I had concluded that there was no relation between you two, I contacted the operator of the ferry you used to cross the Mississippi. He confirmed your name, Deputy, and the fact that you were traveling with one Miss Catalina Santé." The sheriff sat back and folded his arms, as if satisfied over a job well done.

"Let me see if I can finish the rest for you," Matthew said. "I had mentioned where I served as a deputy. Once you confirmed that, you inquired about a woman by the name of Santé."

Catalina let out a heavy sigh. The peace from their morning prayer evaporated.

Her shoulders slumped forward. Here she was in the middle of Texas where not a single soul had ever heard of her before, and already the story of what happened back home reared its ugly head. How would she ever escape her past?

"Hey, now." Matthew tried to distract her. "There's no reason for you to be upset. You didn't do anything wrong."

"He's right," Sheriff Durbin added. "I wasn't trying to make it seem like you two were the focus of my investigation."

Catalina looked squarely at the sheriff. "Then why do you care about who I am?"

"It's not so much about who you are," the sheriff spoke softly. "It's more about what trouble you might bring."

"Now hold up just a minute." Matthew leaned forward as he addressed the lawman. "We're just passing through town. Neither one of us wants to bring about any trouble."

"Maybe not, but trouble seems to have followed y'all here just the same."

"Well, that's not my fault – and it certainly isn't hers."

"It doesn't change the fact last night's attack happened."

"Don't remind me." Catalina raised a hand and lightly touched the side of her head. "I'm still feeling the aftereffects."

"Would you like me to call the doctor?" Matthew's tone was filled with genuine concern.

"No. I'll be fine," Catalina quickly answered. Anything was better than drinking more of the doctor's "special blend." The concoction might have eased her pain, but it also clouded her mind. She still couldn't shake off the lazy feeling that plagued her. "It's nothing I can't handle. Besides, I'm really just eager to hurry up and get on our way already."

"That brings me to the heart of the matter," Sheriff Durbin interrupted.

Catalina and Matthew exchanged a look. What now?

"I was thinking that I wouldn't mind traveling with y'all."

"What?" Matthew asked, shock zapping through his veins.

Catalina's mouth hung open.

"We're very flattered," she began. "But I fear we may have already taken up enough of your time."

"And you wouldn't want to leave the town unprotected," Matthew added.

"Nonsense," Sheriff Durbin waved off their excuses. "I've already got a deputy just itching to wear my badge. I'm more than inclined to let him, too. Seems like every other week there's a gunman coming around, trying to prove he's a quicker draw than me. Ain't been licked yet, but I'm sure my time will run out soon enough if I stick around these here parts. Best to get out while the getting's good."

Matthew looked over at Catalina and shrugged. Maybe having another lawman wouldn't be so bad. At the very least, he was added protection should the attacker reappear. He mulled over the idea for a moment, then slowly nodded in agreement.

A twang of disappointment sprouted in Catalina. How could they continue the conversation from earlier with an extra set of ears listening in?

"That ol' town doc of yours said she should take a day to rest." He bobbed his head at her. "A right shame since we had originally planned to leave after breakfast. Maybe get to her grandfather's ranch by nightfall. But I reckon' last night changed all that."

"Oh, no. Let's not change plans," Catalina interjected. "I'll be the first to admit that last night's episode left me more than a little rattled. In fact, I don't think I'll feel quite like myself again until I'm under a permanent roof. So let's not waste any more time being all exposed out on the open road. I say we dine, check out and get on down to Mexico already."

The sheriff flashed a knowing look at Matthew.

He gulped down his pride, her message coming across loud and clear. She didn't trust him to protect her. Not that he could blame her after last night's attack. He should've gone after her.

"I say. Breakfast sounds like a mighty fine idea," the sheriff said. He motioned for the serving girl again. "This here hotel has the best breakfast you can find in all of Texas. They serve up a heaping plate of ham, eggs and cornbread."

Catalina's stomach rumbled, and her eyes grew wide as the serving girl approached. "Well, that's settled. I guess I'll have the breakfast special," she ordered.

Both men requested the same. Then Matthew leaned over and winked at Catalina.

"Maybe you should have one of those 'biscuit baskets' made up again."

She smiled, but it faded when a familiar figure entered the eating area. Thomas Delany!

"So, Sheriff, did you investigate Thomas Delany as well?" she asked.

Both heads turned towards Mr. Delany. The man sat down and bark orders at the help, his voice carrying his demands throughout the dining room.

"I did," the sheriff confirmed. "He seems to check out all right. Has a mine registered to him in Silver City."

"Maybe, but I still don't trust him." Catalina puckered her lips as though tasting something sour. "Something about him leaves a bad taste in my mouth."

"Not at all surprising," the sheriff commented. "Not everyone is as they appear on paper."

The server appeared with the food.

Matthew cleared his throat. "Well, I think we can all draw similar conclusions as to what his character might be. So there is no point spoiling a good meal with further talk of it."

"Well said," the sheriff agreed, picking up his utensils and cutting into a thick slice of ham.

Matthew followed suit, but halted with his fork in midair. He waited for Catalina to bow her head and pray over her meal. He still wasn't quite ready to take the step to do the same. However, thinking about the close call they had experienced the night before, he could now appreciate why someone else might.

Chapter Twelve

"I wonder where they're heading," Catalina said from the backseat. An army tank and a couple of trucks filled with soldiers slowly rolled by their patch off the side of the road. The group silently ate their packed lunches as they watched the young men. Some of them wore serious expressions – as though dreading their mission. Then there were others (probably those who had yet to see the ugly side of war) that were still jovial. There laughter reached back to the Model T.

Unfortunately, their cheeriness did little to lift their spirits. Weary from the long journey, the last half hour of the ride had been in complete silence – the first during the entire trip.

"They're probably going to the same place we are." Matthew pulled over to allow the army to pass – another delay that had turned the twelve hours between Texas and Arizona into a two-day trip.

"I highly doubt that," Sheriff Durbin said, chewing on a piece of juniper as he stared out the front window. "They might end up at the frontier, but I'm pretty sure those boys ain't crazy enough to cross it!"

Catalina sighed, anticipating the unavoidable argument to the rude remark. The two men had been going head-to-head almost since they pulled out of Abilene. First there had been the fight that nearly ensued after Thomas Delany expressed a desire to apologize for any misunderstanding. A small handshake soon turned into a kiss on the back of Catalina's hand. Matthew had bristled, but remained seated.

Until the kiss turned into one too many trailing up Catalina's arm.

She had tried pulling her hand away, but Mr. Delany had encased her fingers in a vice-like grip.

That was when Matthew jumped up and grabbed the cad by the collar. He would have throttled him if it hadn't been for the sheriff quickly addressing the infraction.

"Well, John, it's like I told you before. You're more than free to travel wherever your heart desires. After all, you've got a perfectly good horse back there just going to waste."

The horse had been a sore point since Sheriff Durbin had first surprised the traveling party with a mare that he insisted trot behind the Model T. The poor beast had needed numerous watering breaks. Then her ropes had to be retied to the spare tire when they noticed her trotting off in a lonely direction away from the car.

The added delays could have been foregone had the sheriff sold the horse before they left town. He just couldn't bring himself to part with the solid brown beauty, though. The green-broke was a gift from the folks in Abilene when the good sheriff caught a notorious outlaw during a bank heist two weeks prior. That's when he got the notion of breaking the horse in and riding out of Abilene.

Until Matthew and Catalina arrived – presenting the possibility to leave even sooner.

"Well, if I've told you once then I've told you twice that Abigail's just now taking up a saddle."

"All the more reason she should be wearing one now," Matthew argued. "The best way to break a horse is to ride her."

"So says you," Sheriff Durbin interjected. "I've got my way of doing things, and you've got yours. When it's your horse we're talking about, then you can break her in any which way you want to, Son."

Matthew bristled at the use of the word *son*. The only other man to call him that was his father right before he made it clear that he was no longer interested in being a "family man."

It just wasn't meant to be, Son.

The sheriff wasn't but a couple years older than him. Who did he think he was calling him 'son?' Matthew narrowed his eyebrows and shot the passenger an annoyed glance. "I've broken a horse before, *Boy*, and it didn't include driving ten miles per hour so the horse didn't tire out."

"Don't be sarcastic now, Son. If you've got some sort of need for speed, then I'm telling you she could probably go twice as fast if you'd take that grandpa foot of yours—"

"Enough!" Catalina yelled.

Both men startled and whipped their heads toward the back seat.

Silence. That was better. She tempered her voice. "It has been a long, trying journey for all of us. However, arguing is only going to make us even more irritable than we already are. So, let's all try to be just a little more civil to one another."

Matthew threw a quick smile over his shoulder then refocused his attention on the road. He admired Catalina's grit and durability, qualities a woman would need in Mexico.

"Shall we continue?" he asked.

Catalina looked at him squarely. The tone in his voice was playful, but she could read the challenge in his eyes in the rearview mirror. Deciding to meet it, she sat up a little straighter and raised her head ever so slightly.

She looked out the car window as though without a care and replied, "As soon as this car passes."

Laughter erupted from the front passenger seat. "Watching the two of you in action is even better than seeing one of those moving pictures."

Catalina tried to look offended, but it was pointless. She smiled at the ridiculousness of it all.

"Like the two of you were any better," she replied. "Worse than an old married couple. Bickering over some mule."

"Mule?" The sheriff choked out a cough. "That is good horseflesh, young lady."

Matthew let out a deep, throaty laugh that rumbled throughout the car. It proved contagious, and both the sheriff and Catalina joined in.

"Whoa, now." The sheriff wiped the mirth from his eyes as a fat raindrop hit the windshield. He stuffed the last of a tortilla in his mouth. "We better get back on the road and find some shelter."

Matthew stuck his head out the window and looked up at the graying sky. "Oh, it doesn't look too bad."

"So says you," Sheriff Durbin countered. "Timing has everything to do with the outcome of a rain dance."

Catalina lifted a quizzical brow. "What's that supposed to mean?"

"It's an old cowpoke's saying," Matthew answered for the sheriff. What John's story?

A car whizzed past them. How odd to see another vehicle on this lonely road.

He pulled out behind the car and continued, "It means that if it's meant to rain right now, then it's going to happen – regardless of what anyone says, thinks or does."

"Yep," the sheriff agreed. "That about sums it up."

Silence from the back seat? That was even odder than the other car. Matthew smiled.

"I picked up a few things from my father," Matthew explained. "He was from Arizona."

Catalina picked up on the tone in Matthew's voice. It sounded somewhat bitter.

And he used the word *was*.

Had his father passed away?

The question rested on the tip of her tongue, but how could she pry – especially in front of their traveling companion. Besides, if Matthew had wanted her to know more, then he would have said as much.

"I didn't get to really know him."

Catalina stared at the rearview mirror, hoping to catch Matthew's eyes. She couldn't speak for the judge, but she could promise that she wouldn't judge Matthew based on his past.

He finally did look up.

"My father's family helped him… um… see the *error* in his ways. He petitioned for an annulment right before I made my appearance."

Catalina's mouth dropped in surprise. His father had abandoned him? And to ask for an annulment! No wonder he had a hard time accepting Christ.

An uncomfortable silence seized the group and the sheriff cleared his throat.

"Yep. Just like I said." Sheriff Durbin sat up straighter and readjusted his hat as though preparing for action. "Here comes the rain."

No sooner than he spoke, did the skies open up and unleash a furious downpour on them.

Matthew drove slower, the rain making it difficult to see the road. Would it be better to stop or keep going? A crack of lightning popped off to the right. "Whoa! That was close. We're less than an hour away from Nogales," he informed the other two. "I say we push through."

The horse whinnied from behind as if in protest.

"And I say we don't," the sheriff argued. "Abigail needs some shelter right now."

"Don't worry," Matthew replied. "Horses were standing around in rain long before humans came along."

"He's right, Sheriff," Catalina spoke up. "Besides, I think there's the real reason she's getting upset."

She pointed ahead at the lights shining back at them. A car blocked the road, the same one that had passed them, two uniformed soldiers standing sentinel. One was tall and wiry, the other short and stubby. The tall one signaled for Matthew to slow down and pull over to the side of the road.

"What in the world is going on?" Catalina questioned.

"Maybe those boys need some help," Matthew offered a possible explanation.

Sheriff Durbin shook his head in disagreement.

"Then why are they blocking the road? Something's up."

Matthew eased over to the side of the road. "Maybe there was an accident ahead." He was trying to remain positive, but it was difficult while in the midst of a thunderstorm, roadside soldiers, and a prancing horse that mirrored his own anxiousness.

"Here comes one now," Catalina pointed out. "If nothing else, maybe they can help us find a place to ride out the storm."

A young soldier knocked on the car's special-made window (a rare attribute that few requested). He motioned for Matthew to open the door, who did as requested while the other passengers eagerly awaited.

"Afternoon, sir." A young soldier who looked barely old enough to serve nodded at them, his Southern accent thick. "I'll have to request that y'all step out of the automobile."

"Good afternoon, soldier. I'm Deputy Martin. What seems to be the problem here?" Suspicion crawled through his belly and he glanced over to John. The sheriff fingered the butt-end of his pistol.

The soldier shifted and looked over his shoulder to a man standing beside the other car.

What was going on? Warning bells sounded in Matthew's head. Something was off. His fingers curled around the door handle.

"Excuse me, sir." The soldier put his hand on the door to keep it from closing. "As I've already stated, you and your friends will need to step out of the vehicle. The torrential rains have caused some unexpected flooding ahead, and it is too dangerous to cross."

Matthew peered ahead at the small dip. Maybe there could be some flooding. Otherwise, the land looked relatively flat.

He met the sheriff's disbelieving glance. No. Something was definitely wrong. "Well, in that case, I think we'll just turn back around."

Matthew began closing the door again…until a pistol waved in his face.

"Whoa, son." The sheriff quickly fingered his own firearm.

"Don't even think about it, or your friend here gets a face full of shot." The boy sneered at Sheriff Durbin while thrusting the gun into Matthew's face. Matthew gritted his teeth and instinctively reached for his own gun.

"*Yo no haría eso si fuera tú. ¿Entiendes?*" One of the other men had gotten out of the car that blocked the road. He warned Matthew from drawing his firearm as he approached.

Matthew noted the army uniform, but it was obvious that he didn't serve in the United States Army. Everything about the man – his face, walk, speech – declared he was clearly Mexican.

"Yeah, I understood you just fine." Matthew spat back, his English suddenly tinted with a Spanish accent. "Here's the thing, though. You're not me and I'll do what I very well please!"

Pushing the car door open, he shoved the young soldier a step back who lowered the pistol from Matthew's head.

Matthew planted a boot firmly in the man's stomach.

Sheriff Durbin climbed out the opposite side of the car and withdrew his pistol just as one of the men rushed forward and tackled him. He landed on his back with a solid thud, the gun sliding out of his hand and becoming lost somewhere under the car.

Matthew reached for his weapon. He barely freed it from the holster when a shot rang through the air.

The bullet whizzed past his ear and landed in the car with a sharp pop.

Catalina screamed.

Crouching behind the seat, she stayed low as she climbed out to check on Matthew.

"Stay down," he yelled.

The horse neighed and danced, rocking the car back and forth in her agitation. The horse reared, her powerful legs slamming the back of the car.

"Abigail!" the sheriff yelled. He turned and gave his attacker a concrete kick.

The man screamed and fell to the ground, clutching his knee.

The sheriff grabbed onto the rope holding Abigail just as she broke free.

"Wait, girl!"

The horse tore away. Refusing to let go of the rope, Sheriff Durbin went flying through the air.

"John!" Matthew called out as the horse dragged the man away into the Arizona desert.

The sound of more gunfire caught his attention then, but it was too late.

"Matthew!" Catalina screamed.

The force of the bullet slammed into Matthew, whirling him around. He fell back against the car then dropped to the ground.

She climbed out and sank to her knees beside him, using her skirt to staunch the bright red spot growing on his shoulder. "No, no, no!"

A hand gripped her arm and yanked her away from Matthew.

"Let go of me!" she demanded. She raised a hand and brought it down against the man's round face. The slap stung her palm, but only caused the man to laugh.

He grabbed an arm and tried to drag her towards the other car.

Fingers curled into a fist, Catalina aimed to land a hard right jab on his face.

The man deflected her swing, snagging her wrist before the punch could do any damage. His lips curved, revealing two rows of crooked, yellow teeth.

Catalina cringed.

"I have a special way of dealing with ladies like you," he sneered and hurled her into the backseat of his car.

Catalina scooted to the opposite side, but the other men climbed into the vehicle, blocking her hasty exit.

She gasped and jerked a head over her shoulder.

Matthew lay slumped against their Model T.

"*Agárrala*," he commanded one of the men to hold her.

Strong arms pinned her in place. Her abductor pulled out a white handkerchief then splashed some liquid on it.

Catalina squirmed and managed another glance out the back window.

Matthew hadn't moved. Was he alive? Would he survive the gunshot wound? He needed medical attention now!

The cloth came down over her mouth and nose. She shook her head in an attempt to breathe against it.

Then everything went black.

Chapter Thirteen

Nogales, Sonora, Mexico

It's all a bad dream.

Bad things happened sometimes, but *this* many bad things all at once? Had to be a bad dream. A nightmare. All she had to do was wake up, and she'd be back at home in her own bed, right?

She fought the dream-like place between sleep and awake. *Just open your eyes. You can do it.*

Except she couldn't.

Her arms wouldn't cooperate, either.

So she was not only blindfolded, but her hands were bound behind her back. And so tight! She tried to move a little, but the rope rubbed a raw spot on her wrists.

Panic quickly shot through her, and her pulse quickened. She took in several deep breaths to quiet her racing heart. Her nose filled with dirt and dust tickling her throat.

Afraid to breathe much less cough, she clamped her mouth shut and perked her ears for any sound.

There. A panting. Definitely not her. She stiffened and uttered a silent prayer for courage and strength, and for Matthew.

Why didn't the person say anything?

"I know you're there." She tried to feel around behind her back and her hand landed on something cold and hard. Outlining the shape, she knew it to be a rock belonging to a wall behind her. She tried to push herself up against it. "Why are you doing this? What do you want from me?"

Nothing except more…panting?

A dog? And was that a yawn? Would the guard dog prove to be a foe or friendly? Was escape an option?

If only I could get free of these ropes.

Sitting up as much as she could, Catalina maneuvered her palms along the brick wall.

Crumbling. Jagged. Maybe she could use a sharp edge to free her!

Her pulse raced, excitement and fear swirling together in her belly. She rubbed the rope against the sharp edge. The bonds burned into her skin, searing pain shooting through her wrists. Catalina winced.

Just think of something happy. Mama sewing a new dress. Papa stocking the shelves. Adam hiding her church shoes on Sunday morning. Matthew…

The momentary flashes of happier times were fleeting. Thinking about them only made her feel worse. Especially when she began to think about the roses Matthew had gotten just for her.

Hot tears trailed down her cheeks. So much for thinking of happier times. But what else could she do? She bit down on her lip to keep from screaming out, frustration and pain blinding her.

What if she screamed? Would anyone rescue her?

A doorknob rattled. Her head automatically turned toward the sound.

Then the door creaked open.

She sat very still.

"So you're finally awake? That is good." A man with heavily accented English mutilated the words. "I'm going to take this off you."

Thick fingers fumbled against the back of her head until the blindfold came undone. She squinted against the light that streamed into the room from four tiny windows that lined two of the walls then focused on the man.

He was probably about the age of her father and almost twice his size. As he stretched to his full height and looked down at her, she could see that height didn't help his portly nature any.

He shoved one hand in his pocket and motioned with the other. "You know what? You look like a sly one to me." He fingered a shaggy mustache and nodded his head as if in agreement to something. "Yes. You feel like trouble to me."

He paused as though waiting for Catalina to confirm or deny his observation.

She refused to give him the satisfaction.

"Okay." The man clapped his hands together. "Here's what we do. You do as Belmonte says when he says to do it. In exchange, I will untie you and give you the freedom of all of Jericho."

"Who is Belmonte?"

The man looked offended. "Me, of course. Who did you think?" He brandished a long blade in front of her face.

She gasped and shrank back, curling into herself. Oh, Lord, help me!

He laughed, something loud and evil, then pulled her close. Her breathing stilled as he sliced through her ropes.

Catalina rubbed her arms, wincing.

He jerked her to her feet, steadying her when she swayed.

While certainly much fatter than her father, it turned out he wasn't really that tall after all. She easily towered a good inch or more over the man. Odd how such a simple detail gave her a little satisfaction, especially given her circumstances. "So what is Jericho?"

Belmonte shuffled over to the door. With his hand on the knob, he motioned her closer.

Catalina didn't move.

"Don't take all day!" he hollered.

She startled and forced her legs to do his bidding, halting by his side.

He pushed the door open, brandishing his arm through the air, his voice beaming with pride. "This is Jericho."

Catalina stared down a small hallway that led into a crowded saloon.

He motioned for her to precede him into the hall.

She crept past the vile man, dread dogging her steps. She made it to the entrance of the saloon.

Several men sat at old, splintered tables, some playing cards, others just drinking, ladies hanging about their necks, or even sitting on their laps. A distinct musty smell assaulted Catalina's nose. Alcohol!

Alarm pitted in Catalina's stomach. She spotted the front door to the establishment.

"Don't even think about it," Belmonte hissed from behind her.

Catalina turned around and looked down at the little man.

"I'm not afraid of you," she said, defiance lifting her chin.

The man sighed and rolled his eyes. He looked a little amused as he shook his head and said, "Definitely a troublemaker."

Belmonte snapped his fingers and motioned from behind her.

"Here is what is going to happen," the man said. "You are going to stay here and make my customers happy. Not very happy since your benefactor has set out some rules for you. Still, you can do other things within reason." The man gestured at the throng of men, who now stared at her, greedy and hungry, as if they would devour her for lunch.

"No," she cried. "I'm not staying here."

"Yes, you are because that's how things work here."

Catalina backed away from Belmonte only to be snatched up by a brawny man. He threw her over one of his shoulders and headed toward a set of stairs.

"*LET... ME... GO!*"

She pummeled the man's back with her fists and kicked her legs, trying hard to injure the man. He didn't even flinch.

He hauled her up the stairs and kicked open a door. Entering the modest quarters, he flung her like a sack of flour onto a hard bed. She landed on a thin mattress with a grunt, then watched as he sauntered out of the room – big as you please – and closed the door behind himself.

Catalina jumped up and raced after the man, twisting the knob. Locked in! She pounded on the wood, splinters cutting through her skin. "Help me, please!"

Her yelling soon turned into sobs and large, wet tears ran down her cheeks. She crumpled into a heap at the bottom of the door.

"That won't help you."

Catalina looked up, startled to see a young woman about her age sitting on a second bed in the corner of the room.

"My name's Mercedes."

"You speak English," Catalina stated plainly.

"Of course I do," the woman rebuffed. "We aren't but a couple of streets from International Boulevard. With all the business and travelers between here and there, just about everyone in this pueblo can speak both English and Spanish."

Catalina fumbled for an apology. "I'm sorry. I wasn't trying to be rude. It's just that I figured since this is Mexico, everyone only spoke Spanish. It's really nice to meet someone I can talk to, though." Could this woman help her? And why was she here?

"Well," Mercedes impatiently placed her hands on her hips. "Aren't you going to tell me your name?"

"Oh, I'm sorry," She stood up and held out a filthy hand. "I'm Catalina Santé. Well, not really. I mean, I am, but that's not my family's real name." Stumbling over her explanation, she shook her head and stopped.

Mercedes stared at the outstretched hand for a moment. Then she took a firm hold and pumped it one good time.

"Welcome to Jericho."

"What exactly is this place?" Catalina raised a questioning eyebrow and glanced around the sparse room. A small table with two chairs sat beside her; a tall wooden dresser with a mirror on the door occupied the opposite corner.

"Jericho. The cantina where *everything* is for sale. The drinks cost four pesos. But if a man buys a woman a drink, it costs him eight pesos, and requires a particular woman to sit with him and keep him company."

"But don't the women get drunk?" Catalina shuddered. Surely the alcohol would be as bad (or worse) than the doctor's concoction. Nausea settled into the pit of her stomach.

"Some do," Mercedes explained, "but that's only because they want to. Most of us know how to play cat and mouse with these animals. All you do is act like you're sipping your drink. Then you excuse yourself to go to the wash closet, bring your drink with you and pour most or all of it out. It makes it necessary for the men to buy you another drink."

"But why would you want them to?"

"Because the women are supposed to get half of all the money they help bring in so that they can buy their freedom one day. The other half goes to the owner, Señor Belmonte."

Disgust and revulsion trembled through Catalina. How horrible!

"Then there's always the ultimate purchase - buying a woman's affections. A man does that and she's his for the entire night. Señor Belmonte allows the women to choose their own rate."

"What's the highest rate?"

"Well, Eloisa is the highest paid at fifty pesos. But you're prettier than she is, so you'll probably be able to ask more."

Catalina let out a gasp, horrified. "What? Honestly, Mercedes. I don't plan on anyone buying me a... a tortilla, let alone paying for something so sacred. I'm a

Christian and there are certain principles I hold to. And just to make sure none of these men get any bright ideas, I plan to be so disagreeable and ask so much money that they'll change their minds."

"Well, you're not like the rest of the women here anyway." Mercedes sighed. "Someone is paying to have you kept."

Paying to have her kept? That was ridiculous! Who would do that? "How do you know that?"

"Oh, I know everything that goes on around here." Mercedes smiled at her and winked. "I'm kind of considered *la señora* of the house."

"You're the lady of the house?" Catalina asked, surprise wobbling through in her voice. How could that be? The woman couldn't be more than a few years her senior.

Mercedes shook her head. "I know what you're thinking, and, no. I'm not married to Belmonte. They just call me that since I've been here the longest, and I kind of take care of the girls."

Catalina nodded as though she understood, but that was far from the truth. She shook her head, massaging her temples. As if that would rouse her from this horrible nightmare! "Listen," she began. "You say you take care of the girls. So maybe you can help me."

"Absolutely not." She waved Catalina off. "Don't even think that escaping is possible."

"But I'm not even supposed to be here," Catalina protested. "Even Belmonte said that I couldn't make his customers *very* happy. See? I'm not that kind of girl."

"That would scare me even more because you already have a handler, but you don't know who it is or why. So you don't know what their real intentions are. At least the rest of us know that if we stick to the saloon's arrangements, then it really will help us make money."

Catalina drew her brows together. Her life up until now hadn't prepared her for this harsh reality.

"It's true," Mercedes continued. "In fact, there was once a girl who met her husband right here in this bar. Oh, it was like a fairytale. The man loved her so much that he wanted to marry her and take her away from here. So he paid Belmonte ten thousand pesos and off they rode into the sunset."

Catalina began pacing. How revolting that a man would presume to buy her hand in marriage. And after degrading her in such a vile way!

"I refuse to make a cent - or a peso - in such a humiliating manner. I will use everything in my power to disappoint the handler for…selling me!" She could hardly bring herself to say the word. She would show him that she was high maintenance and not worth the trouble. Then maybe he'd let her go.

"Hmmm. I guess we will see about that." Mercedes moved to stand in front of the large, plain wardrobe. She buried her head inside and pulled out a ruffled black skirt and white shirt. "Belmonte likes the girls to look nice. So change into this."

Catalina waved her hand through the air. "I'm sorry, Mercedes, but I—"

"Don't say you don't want it, because another girl did and I haven't seen her since that day. So get changed and then come with me. I'll introduce you to the other girls around here, and we'll help you make a new home for yourself. *Sí*?" Mercedes didn't wait for an answer, but returned to the makeshift vanity and began pulling out various tubes of rouge and lip paint.

Did she really mean to plaster all that makeup on her face?

A tremor started in her toes and worked its way up to her torso. She wrapped arms around her chest. How had she gotten into this mess, and how was she to get out?

Catalina stared at the outfit, tears pricking her eyelids. Was Mercedes serious about some girl disappearing for refusing to wear the clothes Belmonte dictated? Or was it an idle threat?

Why, God? Why is this happening? Will I ever get out of here? Will I get to see Matthew again?

Is he even alive?

Chapter Fourteen

"Papa! *Ya se mueve!*"

Matthew understood the woman as she called out for her father. The fact that someone was watching him and reporting his every move motivated him to open his eyes. Bright light pained his sight as he brought the room into focus. The whitewashed adobe walls and thick oak beams reminded him of his childhood home.

He groaned as he rolled to his side and tried to sit up.

"*Relájate, Hijo.*" A hand landed on his shoulder and gave a gentle push back toward the bed.

"Thanks for the concern, friend," He realized that the Spanish word for son didn't rub him as raw as it did when he heard it in English. It must have been because it was part of everyday language in Mexico. A term of endearment instead establishing authority. "I have a gang to catch."

"The ones that did this to you?" The man gestured towards Matthew's head.

Matthew touched his head, expecting matted blood or a huge bump, surprised at the bandage wrapped around it.

"Must've happened during the shootout." He shifted and groaned. His head pounded, vicious and unforgiving, and nausea threatened to embarrass him in front of the kind man. He took a deep breath, planted a palm on the mattress, and tried to sit up.

Oh. That was a mistake. He dropped back onto the bed, weak as a rag doll.

"I told you to relax," the elderly gent reminded him, empathy etching lines in his leathered cheeks.

Matthew lifted a hand and covered his face as though he could wipe away the shame of appearing so weak.

"I know, I know."

He removed his hand from his eyes and looked around. "Where am I anyway?"

"My ranch." The man flashed a kind, proud smile. "My daughter has been taking care of you for two days now."

"Two days!" Matthew winced. Those *banditos* were probably long gone by now. "I've got to get out of here."

He struggled to push himself up again. With the man's help, he swung his legs over the side of the mattress and sat.

"Thank you, señor. I'm grateful for the medical attention and for your daughter's kindness, but I must be going now." Matthew shoved off the edge, bracing a palm against the wall, as he steadied himself on his feet and glanced around for his boots. "I suppose I owe you my life." He offered an outstretched hand.

The man grabbed hold of it, his grip firm and full of vitality. "It was nothing, *Hijo*. Besides, it was really my daughter, Amorina, who saved your life." He motioned to the young woman who stood a few feet away. "She found you on the side of the road. You still had a little strength then, and she helped you into our buckboard and brought you here."

Matthew looked over at the young woman, and nodded his gratitude. "Thank you."

Amorina shyly hung her head. "It was, um, it was…" she struggled for the right words, "my pleasure."

"My daughter doesn't speak very much English," the man apologized.

"Esta bien," Matthew assured him that it was all right. "I speak Spanish. *Gracias por su ayuda. Me llamo Mateo Martín.*" He introduced himself by his Spanish name.

Amorina nodded again. Then, as though suddenly remembering, she gestured towards her father. "This is my father, Papa Juan."

The man grabbed Matthew's hand and shook it a second time. "Oh, excuse me. There has been so much excitement around here that I almost forgot. My name is Juan Rangel."

Matthew rubbed his forehead, trying to clear the fog. There was something familiar about that name, but he couldn't remember what it was. He shook off the thought and scrounged up a smile for Juan.

"Again, I thank you – both of you – for saving my life. However, I need to be on my way."

Matthew took a cautious step, reaching a hand out to the headboard as a wave of dizziness washed over him.

"I'm sorry, *mi'jo*, but I don't think you're going anywhere anytime soon."

Matthew gritted his teeth. "This can't be happening. I can't waste another second lying in bed. I've got a gang to track down!"

The man studied Matthew for a moment. A serious look crossed his face. "Listen, my son. You have sustained many bad injuries. If you don't let them heal, then they could become worse – even infected." The man rested his hand on one of Matthew's shoulders. "Is chasing a gang really worth risking your life?"

"It is if I catch up to them," Matthew replied.

"Why? Why is it so important for you to catch this band of outlaws?"

Matthew gave the man an incredulous look. "It's important for the safety of every man, woman and child of the Southwest territory. We can't allow another raid to happen like the one at Columbus. I have to catch the men responsible!"

Juan's bushy eyebrows shot up, his bewildered gaze skidding between Matthew and his daughter. "Why do you speak of that old battle? Those men aren't around anymore."

"Not around anymore? What are you talking about?" Matthew asked, trying to ignore the twin faces and the spinning room.

The man repeated what he said. "You know. Most are dead. Others in jail."

"That's impossible." Matthew rubbed the bandage, sifting through the fog that was his brain for answers. "What day did you say it was?"

"Saturday." The elderly gentleman then spouted out the date.

Matthew sank back down on the mattress, elbows on his thighs, hiding his face in his hands.

Nineteen eighteen. How can that be possible?

And why couldn't recall the last two years of his life?

Chapter Fifteen

"See? You don't look so bad."

Catalina swung around to look at Mercedes, who casually leaned against a standing mirror. A single glance at her reflection and Catalina cringed. With the dress snuggly fitting her figure, she had a commanding *take-me-I'm-yours* look. She tugged the front of the dress down, but the hemline insisted on remaining just above her knees while the back swept down to the floor in a faux train style. The sleeves had been shortened as well, stopping right under her elbows – leaving the rest of her arms bare for all to see.

They were also trimmed in red to draw more attention. If that didn't work, then the red sash tied around her hip certainly would.

"Like I said," Mercedes smiled. "Not too bad."

Catalina shook her head. "I'm sorry to be so disagreeable, but this simply won't do."

"What do you mean it won't do? What do you think? You have a choice or something?"

Exasperated, Catalina threw her hands up in the air. "Well, I just can't go out there looking like this!"

"Well, what do you think you're going to go out looking like?"

An idea took root then blossomed. Catalina smiled, grabbed Mercedes's arm. "Come on. I'll show you."

"Oh, come on. It ain't like anybody's gonna care what you look like."

John stood beside the military truck looking like a disheveled site. There was dirt all over his arms and a large hole in the seat of his trousers. Abigail had dragged him through the desert until she had worn herself out. Fortunately, his long walk back to the car in the sweltering heat crossed the path of a couple of soldiers.

Real soldiers. Thank God!

Unfortunately, it didn't look like Abigail was much for cooperating. She wouldn't allow herself to be tied or mounted.

John took another step towards Abigail. He hoisted the saddle in the air and held it out like a prize. "Just think of it as an early Christmas gift."

The horse neighed and backed up. John took a few steps closer. The movement irritated the animal and she stomped a hoof in warning.

"Sorry, Sheriff, but I don't think you're gonna' get that there beast to do what you want."

John ignored the soldier.

"I think you mentioned that before… And it may be, but I happen to disagree." John reached into a saddle bag that he'd pilfered from the abandoned Model T and pulled out a bright red apple. "All this little gal here needs is a little sugar. Ain't that right, sweetheart?"

John waved the apple and clucked at her. The horse swished her tail then took a cautious step forward. Sniffing out the apple, she lifted it from his hand and chomped.

As she stood chewing, John inched his way close to her and eased the saddle over her back, the leather only skimming her hair. She reared up again.

"Whoa, girl!" He shouted to be heard over the soldier's laughter. Then he remembered just who he was talking to. He clucked a few times, then spoke soft. "We have a job to do, Abby. We've got to find our friends before them *banditos* do something bad to them."

The first soldier sobered at the mention of Mexican bandits.

"What are you talking about? You said the horse dragged you away during an attack on your car. You never mentioned anything about bandits taking off with anyone."

"Well, that's what they were. They attacked me and my friends – shot at one of them actually. It about made Abigail have a nervous breakdown."

"Abigail?" The second soldier questioned.

"Yeah," John thumbed back at his horse. "Abigail."

The two soldiers exchanged looks.

John recognized the skepticism.

"Lookie here," his voice grew thick with emotion. Who knew how much time his friends had left? It was time to stop lollygagging! "I'm not crazy. Everything I'm telling you is the Gospel truth! Someone pulled over this here car that I was in. Then they shot at me and my friends, and that made Abigail tear out of there faster than a city-slicker runs from a brawl."

The first soldier rolled his eyes and sighed. "Tell you what. We've got to report back to Lt. Col. Herman. You can come with us and tell him your story."

"Yeah," the second soldier interrupted. "He should be the one to decide if it's a matter for the army anyway."

John nodded in agreement. The longer they dallied, the more danger his friends could be in. "I think speaking to this lieutenant of yours is exactly what I need to do." John repositioned the saddle in his hands and faced Abigail again. He stared at the horse, determined. His jaw clenched.

"Now let's try this again."

Chapter Sixteen

Matthew squeezed his eyes shut and winced as the wagon jostled.

I'd rather be shot with a dozen bullets than sit here a minute longer.

Except that wasn't entirely true. He wouldn't *really* want to be shot with even one bullet – especially if it was like the ones he received. There would be a permanent scar on his shoulder. And he didn't even want to think about how his head would look after a bullet had grazed it.

"*Te gusta?* You like the idea?" Amorina snapped the reigns against the horse as she asked Matthew what he thought about her plans for life. They were all about finding a good husband, having children, and spending the rest of her life taking care of her family and home.

He picked up on her implications and inwardly cringed – still managing a pleasant nod.

"I suppose it sounds good."

Does this horse go any faster?

The distance between town and the small ranch was a little over a half hour, but Amorina's constant chatter about marriage made the ride stretch on forever. Her efforts to try to solidify some sort of relationship between them left Matthew feeling sad for her. After all, she had proved to be a great nurse over the past two weeks. She was easy on the eyes, too. Round in all the right places and so willing to serve. Any man would be happy to make her a bride.

Except Matthew.

The obvious desperation to get married turned Matthew off to any notion of a relationship with her, although he could understand why she so frantically sought a husband. From what he witnessed, Juan was a strict father who expected nothing less than perfection from his daughter.

And it seemed like he wanted the same from a son-in-law, too.

The man seemed kind – almost subservient during the first week of Matthew's stay. However, the man's attitude (and behavior) had shifted over the last few days.

There were small nuances at first that might have gone unnoticed to an untrained eye. However, Matthew was a deputy.

That much he did remember.

He also remembered how he had been taught to pick up on the nuances of tone variations and subtle changes in body language. He could tell when a person was lying or otherwise not all that they seemed.

And he could pinpoint the exact moment he went from "guest" to "family" on Juan's ranch. One moment he was moseying around the ranch. The next? Well, he had picked up just about every strenuous chore possible. Meanwhile, the "old" man complained about his back shortly after the sun came up, and disappeared over the hills to do who knows what.

"Yes? Is good to do?" Amorina interrupted Matthew's thoughts.

He smiled, but stared at the road, not meeting her gaze. Did she realize that he hadn't heard a single word in the last five minutes? Probably not. The woman chattered nonstop.

"Uh… *Si. Esta bien.*" Matthew agreed, finally putting an end to the conversation. "I'm sure it'll be just fine."

She beamed at him and slapped the reigns against the horse with excessive enthusiasm. What had he just agreed to?

Whatever it was, he was grateful for the silence that settled over them for the first time since they left the ranch.

Catalina picked the dry *masa* flour from her raw hands, exhaling with each prick of pain that seared through her palms all the way up to her fingertips. She tried to ignore the intense heat that radiated up her hands, but that was impossible.

Sniffling, two fat tears rolled down her flour-stained cheeks.

"*Ay, no seas chillona!*" Mercedes hissed, shooing her away from the *prensa*.

"I'm *not* a crybaby!" Catalina shot back. However, she gladly moved away from the wooden press that they were using to make tortillas. Storming away to the other side of the small outdoor kitchen, she leaned against a wooden slat that made up part of the wall. Her rebellion against the saloon owner's dress code had sentenced her to servitude.

Tearing off the bottom of her traveling dress and donning the traditional Mexican blouse with the red *rebolso* tied around her waist hadn't impressed

Belmonte. The makeshift sash was still a little too tight for Catalina's liking, but at least she wasn't showing off her legs like the rest of the women.

One look and Belmonte had growled, "You want to look like a servant? Okay. Then I treat you like one."

He'd banished her to work alongside "La Fea," the ugly one, at the wooden *pileta* that doubled as a wash bin for the girls to bathe in. She had knelt beside it for endless hours scrubbing the clothes for the other women, as well as Belmonte, his guards, and the men who paid to spend the night.

Then she was sent to the kitchen to try to whip up Mexican delicacies she could never contrive.

No wonder Jericho thrived during a time of war. Some of the male patrons who visited were American soldiers. What man wouldn't prefer the warm sheets of a clean bed and soft arms of a beautiful woman over a muddy ditch?

They ignored her pleas for help. Didn't care that she was an American held against her will; some even accused her of lying. All they seemed to care about was being serviced, having clean clothes, plenty of alcohol and hot meals. They were eager to buy into Belmonte's claim that she was there to work off her debts from a former employer after being caught stealing priceless silver utensils…

"After years of treating her like part of the family – even educating her like a daughter… Which of course is the reason she's not for sale."

Catalina shook her head in disgust and strode towards the kitchen door that had been left open to allow some of the heat out as they made tortillas.

"Where are you going? The gate is closed, *nena*."

"I kind of learned that a couple of weeks ago, Mercedes." Catalina couldn't corral the sarcasm.

Her back ached. She could barely move her fingers. Her eyeballs burned, and her head banged out a rhythm that would make a drummer jealous. She was tired. So tired from this role that had been thrust on her. She had little patience left to play nice to a woman who acted more like a bully than a friend. "I've walked this courtyard enough times to realize that there's no way to climb over the walls, either. I'm just getting some fresh air, *little girl*." She couldn't even work up satisfaction over turning Mercedes's words back on her.

"More like being a *floja* again."

Lazy? Heat flooded Catalina's face and her fists clenched at her sides. *Lazy?* How dare the woman speak such a lie!

She jerked to a stop at the door, her posture stiff, chest barely moving. Should she confront Mercedes for all the name calling over the past two weeks?

She forced herself to breathe. In. Out. In. Out. Closed her eyes and prayed for strength, for patience, for wisdom. She trusted that salvation would come if she just put her trust in the Lord. Still, she couldn't help but question why this was happening to her. Was this because of the incident with Ben?

At least the men who abducted her had grabbed her satchel, and after inspecting it, Belmonte allowed her the contents. The toiletries and Bible held no value to him. She'd bartered the toiletries, and God's word brought her solace each night.

Of course, Belmonte confiscated the money her mother had given her at the start of the journey so she couldn't bribe one of the soldiers to help her escape.

Home.

It seemed like such a faraway place. Would she ever see it again? Would she ever hug her mama again?

The metal gate at the end of the enclosed courtyard made a loud creaking sound, forcing Catalina's eyes open.

Two of Belmonte's guards ushered in a small group of children. She counted five girls and two boys. Not a one of them looked older than maybe eight years old.

And all precious.

"Why are they here?" Catalina called over her shoulder to no one in particular. But if she was honest with herself, she already knew the answer. She angled around, waiting for confirmation, horror churning in her belly.

"Who?" Mercedes asked as she continued to press the *masa* into perfectly round tortillas. She peeled one off the press and handed it to La Fea to heat on the *comal*, who laid it on the hot sheet of earthenware and skillfully peeled off another without burning her fingers.

"Them." Catalina replied and pointed at the group of children.

"Mind your own business." The commandment hung firm in the heavy air between Catalina and Mercedes. As if sensing the threat of a fight, La Fea's gaze skittered between them and then continued rolling balls of masa for the press.

"What?" Catalina squared off, facing Mercedes.

How could the woman believe this way of life was acceptable?

Feet, shoulder width apart, and hands firmly planted on her hips, Catalina geared up for a battle. "Do you mean to tell me that you would willingly turn a blind eye to helpless children being exploited?"

Mercedes tossed the dough onto the counter and mimicked Catalina's stance.

"Why not?" she asked. "Everyone seemed to turn a blind eye when it happened to me."

At Mercedes's confession, Catalina recoiled, her hand flying up to cover her open mouth. "Were you very young?" she asked, her voice barely above a whisper.

Mercedes let out a slow sigh. She wiped her hands on the apron and shrugged.

"Not as young as La Fea," she said with a small nod at the other woman.

La Fea ignored the comment and continued to turn the bubbling tortillas.

"So how old were you?"

"I had just turned fifteen." Mercedes walked past Catalina and leaned in the doorway as she watched the last of the children. "That's when I became a woman… and a burden on my family."

"A burden? How could your family consider you a burden?"

Mercedes shrugged. "Well, that's what you are when you're one of twelve siblings with nothing to offer."

"I'm sure that's not how they really thought of you. Besides, there isn't much a fifteen-year-old girl *can* offer anyone at that age."

Mercedes shook her head in disagreement. "You still don't understand how things work, *nena*."

"Then explain it to me." Catalina crossed arms over her chest and raised a challenging brow. She had seen some ugly situations ever since she arrived at

Jericho. Even her own station of servant wasn't a secure one. One – or more – of the men could try to corner her at any time. She had seen it happen to several of the women already.

Taking advantage of children was a different story, though.

One she planned to stop... if she could.

"Look, it's like this. Very few girls here are educated. Hardly any of them can read or even write their own names. So it isn't like they can earn money to help at home."

"And they can't work the land like the boys can," La Fea chimed in. She kept her head down and continued working.

"Exactly," Mercedes continued. "So what do you do with an extra mouth to feed when there isn't any money to do so? You do the next best thing and give her to someone else to take care of."

"So the parents think they're giving their children to people who can take better care of them?" Catalina asked. How was that even possible?

"Yes." Mercedes confirmed. "And usually it's to someone good. If a man comes around looking for a young *señorita*, then he typically wants a wife who is strong enough to bear him a lot of children. So he'll pay her family to have her and it works out for everyone."

"Because now the family can afford to eat and there's one less child to worry about." Catalina finished the line of thought.

Mercedes nodded, sadness etching her lips. "But sometimes it doesn't work out like that." She looked up at the sky and took in a deep breath. She closed her eyes as she spoke again. "Sometimes a man says all the right things and pays the family the money that they need, but then he brings her to a place like this instead of marrying her. Then he can keep making more money on her as she's passed around."

"And what about the children?" Catalina asked, a trace of fear lacing her voice.

"Anything could happen." Mercedes explained. "Maybe a nice American couple who can't have children will adopt them. That's the dream that's sold to their parents who want them to have the chance of a better life."

"But that's not what happens. Is it?" The ugly truth sank like a concrete block in a river, never to see daylight again.

Was that how these children would feel? Some analogy about darkness

The woman slowly shook her head. "It's more likely that they'll be used as house servants." Mercedes paused before continuing. "Or one day they'll be like us."

Catalina was at a loss for words. Mercedes had spoken so highly of her position at Jericho when Catalina first arrived. She made it seem like it was a chosen profession – not a sentence of servitude.

"What about all the money you make?" Desperation weakened her knees, cut off her airways. "Can't you use it to get out of this place?"

"Sure she could," La Fea spoke up. She threw down a tortilla and wiped her hands, anger brewing in her eyes. "She could probably take the money and escape to America to live happily ever after. Of course, Belmonte has to *give* her the money first."

Catalina's gaze jerked to Mercedes.

The same anger that possessed La Fea stiffened the other woman's shoulders and hiked her chin.

"He keeps it all?"

Mercedes smiled, but it wasn't from humor. "Oh, no. He doesn't keep it *all*. He gives us the *pesitos* we need to go to the market and nothing more." Her eyes welled up and the woman swiped her cheeks with the soiled dish towel. "He keeps the rest safely hidden – for our own good, of course."

"But that means—"

Mercedes nodded, sniffling.

La Fea diverted her attention back to the tortillas.

Catalina's stomach plummeted to her boots, fear holding her hostage. She didn't need confirmation to know what that meant.

There was no escape from Jericho.

Chapter Seventeen

The doctor checked Matthew's head, prodding his scalp and lifting his arm, checking for infection.

Amorina peered over the doctor's shoulder, her gaze spearing him as if he were a specimen on display. Why couldn't she give him some space? Both he and the doctor had tried to convince her to remain outside, but she would not budge. Didn't she realize how improper it was for her to be there? It made him feel uncomfortable, too!

"This looks pretty good. All clean, no fever." The doctor nodded with approval. "Seems like you had a pretty good nurse."

"That I did." Matthew agreed, reluctant to acknowledge her but understanding that credit should be given where due.

He looked over at Amorina and she tried to play coy, lowering her head as if embarrassed by the compliment. He sighed inwardly at how she reacted to even the slightest approval.

The doctor must have misread the exchange between the two. He leaned towards Matthew, under the pretense of speaking privately.

Except he purposely failed to lower his voice when he spoke.

"You might want to hold onto that one," he said with a wink.

Matthew stuck his tongue in his cheek. Ignoring the doctor's comment, he used his good hand to fish around a pant pocket for some money.

"How much for today's visit?" he asked.

Amorina quickly stepped forward and addressed the doctor. "My father asked that you bill him any charges for today's services." The words came out perfectly, as though rehearsed quite a bit.

An uncomfortable feeling took up residence in his chest. "I'd prefer to pay my own bill. Thank you for the offer, though." He held out a wad of bills for the doctor.

"No." She held her hand over his. "He insists that he repay you for the work you've done."

Matthew saw through the farce. The work he had done around the small ranch was laborious, but hardly equaled the doctor's bill when factoring room, board and nursing services.

Either the girl or her father intended that Matthew become indebted to them. He wanted no part of that type of arrangement. It was past time for him to move on.

The doctor glanced between them, uncertainty on his face.

Matthew shoved the money into the doctor's hands. "Like I said, I prefer to pay my own way through life. Besides, you and your father have done more than enough for me."

Amorina's shoulders drooped, and her lower lip jutted out.

He despised hurting the woman, any woman, but especially one who had gone out of her way for him to like her.

Still, he just couldn't find any other way to keep her from getting her hopes up. She wanted more from

Matthew than he was willing to give. The look of adoration never seemed to leave her eyes.

"Thank you, Doctor." Matthew shook the physician's hand and exited the small clinic.

Like a puppy following her master, Amorina trailed, hot on his heels.

"I need to go one more place." She waited for an approving nod. "You come with me?"

Matthew considered offering an arm like any gentleman while walking through town. The streets of Nogales could be dangerous. But, that would give her the wrong impression.

So he shoved his hands in his pockets and walked beside her down International Boulevard, the dirt road that separated the small Mexican town of Nogales from the American one of Nogales, Arizona.

The quaint architecture resonated throughout most of Mexico, tiny in comparison to the ones right over the border.

He returned his attention to the girl when she veered off to one building with a cross hanging outside.

Matthew hesitated. *Do I really want to go inside there?*

He had been thinking about God a lot lately – especially since the gunshot to his head had left his mind a jumbled mess. Flashes of another life – bits and pieces that needed to be pieced together like a puzzle – filled his dreams night after night.

He'd considered praying about the matter, but he and God hadn't been on speaking terms in a very long time.

"You coming?" Amorina paused outside the front door of the church.

Matthew looked up at the cross one more time. Then he took a deep breath. "Right behind you." He stepped inside, exhaled and looked around the room.

Beside the door was a small basin of water. Behind it was a vase with flowers.

Amorina dipped her hand into the water and crossed herself.

An older man in a long dark robe appeared. "*Buenos días, mi'ja.*" The man held out a hand to the girl as he greeted her. She kissed it. "*Como puedo ayudarle hoy?*"

"*Buenos días,* Padre Emmanuel."

Matthew continued to explore his surroundings while his companion explained her reason for the visit. He walked past several rows of pews before choosing one near the altar. A large statue of Jesus on the cross stared back at him.

An urge to pray welled up, soft as a whisper, as gentle as a brush of angel's wings, but the unfamiliar surroundings staunched the words.

His gaze wandered to the Savior, hanging on the cross. No condemnation, even with the nail-spiked hands and feet. Only welcome. Warmth. Grace.

His surroundings faded into the background, unimportant, insignificant, and he sank to his knees.

Bowing his head, he squeezed his eyes shut tight. Words clamored through his brain, fighting for release, but only four made it to the surface.

God, please help me.

Matthew knelt there for a time with his head bowed, chanting the same phrase over and over. No other words broke free. He didn't feel any more enlightened than when he first entered the church.

Had he misplaced his trust? Wasted his time coming in?

A hand landed on his shoulder. "Are you okay, my son?"

Matthew looked up at the priest. A heavy sigh escaped as he rose from his knees and slid into a pew.

"I don't know." He rubbed a hand against his forehead in an attempt to ward off a burgeoning headache. "I've got a hundred different things going through my head. None of it makes any sense."

The priest sat down beside Matthew and adjusted the material of his robe.

"Yes. I've heard of your plight." The priest smiled at his slight startle. "Not too much goes on around here without me finding out about it. Many come to me when desperate or contrite. Even individuals you would think to see only on their deathbed will appear out of nowhere if the circumstances are right."

"I suppose I fall into that last category," Matthew admitted, ashamed to talk to the old man after being away from the church for so long, but he couldn't hold back the truth. "I guess you could kind of say that when it comes to faith, I'm a bit of a work-in-progress."

The priest only shrugged. "We're all a work-in-progress. Not a single one of us is perfect." He paused and looked directly at Matthew. "That's why we need the One who was."

Matthew felt as though the old man's gaze could bore a hole into his soul.

Can he tell what kind of man I am? Can he see where I stand?

"I know all about the One you talk about. I read his story in the Good Book and all." He looked down at his hands and shook his head. "I don't think he'd really want someone like me, though."

"That's not true." Father Emmanuel spoke emphatically. "He wants all of us, all the time."

Matthew wanted to believe that was true, but he knew what kind of man he'd been. Despite his mother's hard work – bringing him to church regularly and trying to raise him right – anger and hate had encased his heart when he learned that his father had abandoned them.

All because they were from the "wrong people."

And he was angry with God for allowing him to be humiliated in front of his father's new family. He had sought out the man – a hopeful teen wishing for the father he had never had. Instead of being lovingly received, he had been ridiculed and turned away.

"You don't understand," Matthew began. If he couldn't confess to a priest, than who could he bare his soul to? "I couldn't even trust the father who helped make me to stick around, and I could *see* him. Why should I believe in some invisible man in the sky? He ain't never proved he cares about me."

"Ay, *hijo*. I think it is you who doesn't understand." Father Emmanuel explained. "You thought that this man whom you wanted to call father so much was the answer. But he wasn't. God is the only answer, and he does care about you. Just think of what the Psalmist wrote, 'Your eyes saw my unformed body; all the days ordained for me were written in your book before one of them came to be.'

The priest paused, allowing Matthew to digest the scripture.

"Do you see now how God's love works? He knew you – *loved* you – before you were even born. So much so that he actually saved all your days to come in His book. Then, as if that wasn't enough, he gave you a gift. It was the greatest gift anyone could ever part with… His only begotten son. That's how much he loves His children. That's how much he loves *you*. We are in the position to be forgiven of all our sins and gain salvation – if we only accept it. Will you accept it, *hijo*? Do you want the Father who will never forsake you?"

A sudden sense of urgency squeezed his chest, and he knew what it was that he wanted – what he *needed* to do.

Bowing his head, he prayed, admitting to the wrong that he had done in the past and asking God to cleanse his heart from all the turmoil he held there. Yes, he wanted his Heavenly Father.

Matthew opened his eyes with a renewed sense of purpose and saw the priest's head also bowed in prayer. He waited, the silence soothing his parched spirit, until the man lifted his head.

"I hope you don't mind that I prayed for you."

Matthew smiled. "Not at all. I'd like to think that God listens to all prayers – mine included."

The priest nodded in agreement. "You would be right," he said as he stood and smoothed out his robe. "Now I think there is another important matter that we need to discuss."

Matthew hoisted himself off the pew and arched a questioning brow. "What's that?"

"Why, we need to discuss the arrangements for your marriage, of course."

Chapter Eighteen

Married?

Catalina set down the rinsed beans. Mercedes and La Fea placed the chipotle chiles aside to dry later. All three women stared with disbelief at Eloisa. The girl had danced her way through the courtyard and burst into the busy kitchen, practically singing the news of her good fortune.

"That's right, *nenas*. I'm getting married. By tomorrow night, I'll be long gone."

"Oh, yeah?" Mercedes placed both hands on her hips and challenged Eloisa. "Says who?"

"Belmonte himself," Eloisa sang. "He told me that the American soldier who always requested my services offered for my hand just this morning. He'll be here for me tomorrow."

"So that means he wants to marry you?" Catalina asked.

"Yes."

"No." Mercedes smirked.

How could she not be happy for Eloisa? Catalina's gaze snapped between the two women shooting evil looks at one other.

"I *will* get married tomorrow." Anger laced her declaration. Eloisa's eyebrows dipped, and fire flashed from her coffee colored eyes. "You're just jealous that no one has ever chosen you – and never will now that you're an old *bruja*!"

Mercedes' lips curled in a snarl. She looked vicious enough to take a bite out of the girl who dared call her an old hag. She took a step towards the girl.

"So what you mean is that he bought you in order to marry you." Catalina picked up the bowl of beans and stepped between the two women. "Doesn't that mean he owns you?"

She looked up at the girl. Would Eloisa understand that she wasn't really free, that she was simply being traded from one owner to another?

"That's my point exactly," Mercedes interrupted and nodded at Catalina.

Thank the Lord the woman stalled her progress towards poor Eloisa, and erased the venom from her face.

"And the reason why I have always refused to be purchased by *any* man. I would rather save up my money and free myself!"

Catalina sadly shook her head. Neither woman seemed to understand that they would never be free. "Don't you get it, Mercedes? Belmonte may have told you that you'll earn enough to buy your own way out of here, but it's really just a lie. Even you said he only gives you a little bit to go to the market."

"I know, but we still have *something* saved up," Mercedes argued, jutting out her chin. "That alone gives me a little hope – and comfort."

"Does it *really* give you hope, Mercedes? Do you honestly think Belmonte will ever decide you've earned enough to buy your freedom?" She turned to the next woman. "And what about you, Eloisa? Did this man ever actually say he loved you? For all you know, he might be looking for a slave. Maybe he's more interested in having someone to cook and clean for him than he is a real wife."

Eloisa gasped and covered her mouth.

She wasn't done yet. Catalina turned on the last woman. "And I know what you're about, La Fea... *La Fea*. Do you really want to be known as "The Ugly One" for the rest of your life? You try to make yourself as unattractive as possible – refusing to fix your hair or even bathe. I know you do it in the hope of repelling the men who come in here, but it doesn't change the fact that you're still treated like an animal."

Silence. The three women traded glances.

"Well, what would you suggest we do?" La Fea demanded. Her usually timid voice was firm with frustration.

"Yes, what is your great plan?" Mercedes asked, crossing her arms in front of her chest. "You stand there judging us and our way of living, but your situation is no better than ours."

Catalina shook her head. "I'm not judging you. I'm just saying that you shouldn't accept how you're being treated." Maybe now was the time for more than talk. Maybe it was time for someone to take action.

She paced the small confines of the kitchen, the other women's curious stares burning into her back. Her old fighter spirit unleashed like a wild animal finally released from her cage.

"The more I think about it, the more positive I am that we should do something to get out of here." Catalina jerked to a stop and pounded a fist against her open palm. She stared down the women – ready to lead a rebellion against the entire saloon if that's what was necessary to escape. "We can do this. We really can. It's going to take more than the four of us, though."

"Wait a minute," Eloisa held up a hand, backing away. "When did I say I wanted a part in your little uprising? I already told you that I'm getting married tomorrow."

"That again." Irritation skittered up Catalina's spine. "I thought we already discussed that."

"No. *You* discussed it." Eloisa looked bored as she shooed Catalina away. "The rest of us just listened."

Catalina huffed and crossed her arms.

"Don't worry about her," Mercedes interrupted. "She'll realize the mistake she made after it's too late."

The woman was right. Squabbling stole precious time. "You're right. We need to focus on more important things – like the actual details of our escape plan." She paused for a moment and looked at the other two girls who (much like Eloisa) seemed less than ready for action. "This time tomorrow, we might be free! Isn't it exciting?"

Mercedes blanched.

"What's the matter?" Catalina stilled. "You look like you've seen a gho—?" She gasped, fiery pain searing her skull.

"Belmonte said you were trouble." El Perro, a saloon hand, whispered into her ear, his breath hot and rancid against her neck.

"Let go of my hair!" Catalina struggled against his strong hold. She stretched out a hand to the other girls, but they only backed away, immersing themselves in busy work.

Catalina panicked. He'd march her straight to Belmonte, who'd keep her locked up for encouraging the girls to rebel against him. She would never escape.

"Wait, wait, wait!" She dragged her shoes against the floor, but he soldiered on, wrapping a beefy arm around her waist.

"Please! I have a deal to make with you."

Greed stopped the saloon hand in his tracks. He loosened his hold enough to swing her around. A set of keys dangled from his neck.

Word around Jericho was that two other men besides Belmonte carried the gate key. Was this her man?

"What kind of deal?" El Perro's gaze travelled the length of her body, lustful and hungry. No different from the other men in Jericho since Belmonte's off-limits mandate.

She refrained from quivering, playing the only card she had left.

Herself.

"You're different than the other men here." She tilted her head, relaxed her expression into a coy smile. "In fact, you seem like the sort that a woman would want to get to know a little better."

El Perro snorted. "You must take me for some sort of fool." He shook his head. "I might not be much to look at, but I'm not stupid. Certainly not dumb enough to think a woman as beautiful as you would come to me willingly."

He wasn't buying it. *Don't overdo. Just enough sizzle and spice to make him doubt.* "That's not true." Catalina patted his hand and then trailed her fingers up his arm to curl around his bicep.

She dipped her head, flashed a shy smile, and leaned in to whisper, "I would much rather be with someone who is kind than handsome."

El Perro puffed up his chest and he wet his lips.

Time to go all in. "Maybe you could show me some kindness this one time, and not turn me in so I could repay the favor later. *Sí, Papí?*" She fluttered her eyelashes, planted her palm against his chest.

A lump crawled down El Perro's whiskered throat. He glanced down at the hand splayed across his chest.

She gritted her teeth and willed her hand to remain steady. Her legs threatened to rebel, but she scrounged up every ounce of willpower. Too many lives at stake for her to turn to mush now.

Finally, he met her gaze. Nodded.

A hallelujah chorus belted out in her head. She jerked her hand away, caught herself just before she swiped her palm against her dress.

"Okay." His eyes glinted with warning. "But you must promise to never again speak to the other women about running away – or they will be punished on your behalf. Agreed?"

"Yes."

"Then I'll come to you later this afternoon. Be ready for me," El Perro instructed, then sauntered off, a definite swagger in his step.

Yeah, right, buddy. Catalina waited until he disappeared into the saloon to let out a grunt of disgust. Being that close to El Perro had made her insides rebel. She swallowed the bile that had stuck in her throat.

Thank You, Lord. That was the only promise he asked of me!

The old hand hadn't picked up on her usage of the word *maybe*. So she hadn't really bartered away her virtue after all.

Still, a strange, rather large man would occupy her room within a couple of hours – one that was easily twice her size and strength.

He was right when he had told her to be ready. She couldn't out-power El Perro.

But she could outsmart him. And she'd have to do so without involving the other women. That had been the agreement.

Catalina paced the courtyard, towards the iron gates that separated her from the rest of the world. She gripped the bars, the hot metal singing her palms.

No point in trying the handle. It was always locked. Still, she gave it a turn to prove herself right.

People walked by, unknowing about what went on behind the iron gate.

Or maybe they did know, but were too afraid to get involved.

A church stood fifty feet away. Would it be a safe haven? A trio huddled outside the small building and she found herself staring at one of them. He reminded her of Matthew. She sighed, a vision of his dark eyes and strong jaw playing like a dream in her head. The real world blurred.

The moment when she tripped and he caught her. The roses he ordered for their dinner table. The way he had carried her injured body. How he had used himself as a shield, ready to take a bullet for her.

Tears threatened to escape.

"Enough!" She commanded herself to get a grip. Matthew wasn't reality. This – her fingers jerked the iron bars – was real. Jericho was the reality. Escape was the answer if she wanted a different one.

She brushed away the tears and decided to focus on what needed to be done next. Pivoting, she was about to walk away when a familiar figure walked away from the church.

Catalina halted, returned to the gate and squeezed her face between the bars. She squinting against the high noon sun.

Impossible. I'm imagining things. That's all.

Catalina put some space between her and the gate and rubbed her weary eyes.

What if it really was Matthew?

She eased her face back into position and refocused. The build, the shift in his walk… that ugly hat that she'd never forget.

She gasped and forced her cheeks tighter against the steel. "Matthew!" She cried out, and shot an arm through the metal bars, waving it with all her might.

Matthew's head popped up, his gaze swinging in all directions before settling on her. He dipped his hat in acknowledgement, as he would to any stranger he met on the street, then extended a hand to help a woman up onto a buckboard. He climbed in next to the woman, flicked the reins and set the wagon in motion.

"Matthew!" she screamed again, but the horses clomped in the opposite direction.

Did he not recognize her anymore? Or had he created another life with someone else already?

A sob escaped her chest. She loosened her hold on the bars and dropped into a heap on the ground.

Where is my hope now, God?

Chapter Nineteen

Matthew bolted upright in bed. His rigid posture attested to the panic he felt. Dropping his head into his hands, he let out a mournful groan.

"Catalina."

He had just dreamt about her and the ordeal they had endured on their journey out west. It all seemed surreal. However, the sound of her name on his lips assured him that it hadn't been just his imagination. And he was sure that he had seen her face just the day before.

Matthew pinched the bridge of his nose, the details of yesterday still fuzzy with the vivid imagery of his dream. When? Where? Or had he only dreamt that as well?

The priest had grilled him over a marriage proposal that had supposedly taken place during some conversation with Amorina. He could only figure that it must have been one of the many times she had gone on and on, and he'd allowed his mind to wander during her droning.

Who would have thought daydreaming could cause so much trouble?

Matthew shook his head to clear the cobwebs.

At the church! Just before he climbed onto the buckboard with Amorina.

That wasn't a dream!

Catalina had pressed her face through the bars, her fingers gripping them; voice almost desperate and face lit with excitement.

Then he'd flicked his head in acknowledgement and climbed up on the wagon. He'd stolen a backward glance.

She'd crumbled into a heap just inside the bars, her arm stretched out and chest heaving with sobs.

As if she had no one else in the world, and he'd flung her hope and salvation back at her. She must have been a prisoner—

A prisoner!

The gate separated her from the outside world, the compound an impenetrable fortress.

He flung the bed covers aside and reached for his pants. How could he have forgotten her kind eyes, the softness of her skin when he held her? He thought about the first time she had tumbled into his arms, the smell of rosewater awakening his senses.

He had to make tracks. Now! He'd formulate a rescue plan on the way, but that would require more manpower than a sole deputy riding in alone. Where was John anyway? He sure could use a sheriff right now. Shoo! An army of sheriffs would be great.

An army of sheriffs?

That's what Matthew needed. An army.

Catalina paced the confines of her straightened room, chewing on her nail until she tasted blood. She spit it out, the damaged cuticle now an angry red.

She would have never done something as unlady-like as biting her nails back home. What did it matter, though? Her once beautiful hands had turned into raw meat that hardened a little more every day. Not too much longer and they would be riddled with callouses. Plus, her current surroundings kept her so on edge that it proved near impossible to will herself still.

Planning an escape certainly didn't help the anxiety any.

"All things are possible with God," Catalina recited the gospel and offered up a quick prayer – something she found herself doing more often the longer she stayed at Jericho.

Still, peace was slow in coming.

She took in a few slow, deep breaths and focused on the list of completed chores.

Floor swept. Rug beaten.

Oh, and how it had taken a beating!

The sight of Matthew riding off with another woman still filled her with rage, and the shock of his cool dismissal made her head reel.

Please, God, help me stay focused. Catalina shook her head and scanned the list.

Drapes shook. Sheets washed.

While she had slaved away at the *pileta,* the other women stood around the *fogón*, heating up tortillas and gossiped about the men who would likely pay them a visit that evening. She felt sorry for them. They seemed content to give away their bodies.

Catalina swiped at the moisture collecting on her cheeks, sympathy swelling for the girls forced into a harem. Another part of her flared with anger at them for their complacency over their situation.

But then, she hadn't lived here that long. Would she end up just like them if her plan failed?

Sniffling, she swiped at her nose and blinked back the tears. No sense ruining her painted face, and she couldn't afford to break down now. El Perro was due to arrive any minute.

The fresh picked flowers poked from an old clay pot, mocking her. Only a few days here and already Jericho had drained her of life. Would she also lose her "freshness" today? Would she end up like Mercedes and the others, a slave to the whim of any man willing to pay the right price?

Thump, thump.

The knocking on the old pine door startled Catalina. Her pulse rocketed, and her hand fluttered to her chest.

You can do this.

The small boost of confidence helped steady her nerves a little.

"I can do this," she muttered, trying to ignore the perspiration beading along her brow. "With God, all things are possible."

God, does that include an escape plan? A little help here, please?

She grasped the door handle, smoothed down her dress, and tugged the door open.

"Good evening." El Perro's deep voice rumbled through the tiny space. He stepped through the threshold without awaiting an invitation.

Catalina bristled, holding her breath until he passed. Good? That depended on the success of her plan.

"Um, good evening. Why don't you have a seat?" She motioned to the bed.

El Perro smirked and planted a heavy hand on her shoulder. "Sit?" He chuckled, his eyes gleaming like a kid in a toy store. "I'm not here to sit around." He fingered the top of her blouse, his gaze dipping to her chest.

Catalina instinctively jerked away from him.

His eyes hardened. "I thought we had a deal." Nostrils flaring, he gritted through his teeth.

Catalina swallowed hard. If she didn't play the part, her situation would worsen. It was bad enough that she was captured. But sullied?

She shuddered. Yes, she could do this. "Of course we do," Catalina tilted her head, smiling as she twirled a curl of hair around her finger. "Wouldn't you want to get your money's worth, though?"

"Payment wasn't part of the deal. Remember?" El Perro took another bold step towards her.

Catalina bit her tongue. Risqué just wasn't in her nature. Maybe a more direct approach would work to her advantage.

"Of course you're not paying," she stated matter-of-fact. "Truthfully? I've never done anything like this before. But, you already know that." She crossed arms over her chest.

El Perro's eyes bulged and his dirty knuckles grazed her cheek.

She stood still, statuesque, determined not to show the man her repulsion.

"Don't worry. I will go easy on you. You will enjoy it so much, and invite me back many times." His lips parted to reveal blackened teeth. He ran his tongue against the top of them.

So a case of the "uglies" wasn't the only reason he was still single. His revolting behavior revealed the real reason the women in the saloon avoided him.

"Well, I can't see the future, so I can't rightly say if that's true or not. What I do know is that this is a little nerve-wracking for me." Catalina wrung her hands. "So would you mind granting me a little privacy while I prepare myself?" She twirled her finger, gesturing for him to turn around.

El Perro shrugged. He peeled off his poncho and tossed it on the bed. His fingers fumbled with the zipper on his pants.

Catalina's eyes widened. Surely he'd oblige—

He threw back his head and laughed, something wicked and vile, but turned until his back faced her.

Thank You, Lord!

Catalina snatched the heavy clay pot that held the drooping flowers, as if just the mere presence of the man in her room was enough to wilt them. Not her. Energized with this golden opportunity, she brought it up high and slammed it down on his head.

The pot shattered into hundreds of small shards.

The saloon hand stumbled and pitched forward, landing smack dab in the middle of her bed like a dead dog.

Oh my...!

Had she done it again? Murdered someone by accident?

She held her breath, waiting for proof of life or death.

The slow rise and fall of El Perro's back indicated that he was still alive.

Thank You, Lord, for that small victory!

Catalina let out her pent up breath, but then urgency spurred her legs into motion. Time wasn't on her side!

From the safety of the opposite side of the bed, Catalina looked the man over again.

Still out cold, but probably not for much longer.

She had to move fast!

She wouldn't get very far wearing clothes that identified her as a saloon hussy. She needed a disguise.

And that would require a pair of pants.

But the only pair in sight were the ones on her detainee.

Grabbing hold of one of El Perro's boots, she grunted and pulled on it hard. It popped off and sent her backward with a hard thud. She lifted her hand to toss the boot to the floor, but the emblem of a golden snake on his boot gleamed at her.

"Ugh!" Catalina hurled the boot across the room and stood back up. She latched onto the other one and tossed it aside as well.

So, he'd been the one to attack her at the Abilene Hotel. In the few weeks that she had been stranded at Jericho, studying boots had never crossed her mind. If she had, then she would have known El Perro's true nature all along.

And would have acted differently around him – making her escape plan impossible.

A plan that was starting to look hopeful.

"Perro!" A voice hollered from the bowels of the saloon, a couple of octaves louder than the piano, raucous laughter and the clatter of whiskey glasses.

Frantic, Catalina grasped El Perro's pant legs and gave a fierce tug. A couple of tries and she held the clothing in her hand, turning her back to El Perro's nakedness.

She dropped the pants on the floor beside her and fumbled with the buttons on her skirt. It felt like what like it was taking an eternity to get dressed when she finally slipped on the faded jeans.

They fit loose enough to hide her feminine form, but she probably wouldn't pass for a boy, either. The blouse gave her away, as did the length of the pants.

"Perro! Donde estás?"

A door slammed.

Quick! It would be a matter of minutes before someone discovered El Perro draped across her bed. With fear fueling her, she grabbed his poncho and yanked it over her head. Then she crammed her feet back into her own boots. The sombrero that hung on the wall added the finishing touch to her disguise.

Several voices floated up the stairs.

She ripped the chain holding the key from around his neck. He moaned.

Catalina froze.

The man didn't jump up and pounce on her.

She fisted the key and dashed to the window, scooping up the red sash from the floor on the way.

She attached it to the end of one of the drapes and tossed it out the window.

Catalina looked down. Her knees wobbled and sweat moistened her palms.

The makeshift rope stopped right above the row of *nopales*.

Ay! Cactus? *Really?!*

She scanned the options, but the sound of approaching voices left her little choice. She gripped the sash, hiked a leg over the sill and rappelled until she hovered directly above the plants.

Catalina kicked off against the wall, launching herself as far out as she could, and released the rope. She landed with a thud on her backside, throbbing and winded, but with hardly the time to wince. Pain arced through her entire body. Ignoring it, she struggled to her feet and raced toward the gate as if the hounds of hell nipped at her heels, clutching the gate key.

Her only hope for home. For life!

She fumbled with the key, desperation making it difficult to slide into the hole. Taking a deep breath, she slowly inserted it and listened to the key click into place.

Freedom.

Catalina flung open the gates. She bolted from the saloon. Teeming with fear, she ran through the town. Passerbys. Curious stares. Muffled voices. Was anyone following her?

Think Lot's wife.

She wouldn't pause to find out. She was running blind, following her instinct towards the church that stood only several yards away.

With a sweaty palm, she twisted the door open then slammed it closed. Panting, she rested a forehead against the cool wood, and closed her eyes, willing her breathing to return to normal.

Normal? As if that was ever a possibility anymore.

She let out a huff, weary bone deep, and listened. So far, so good. The street sounds remained unchanged.

"*Buenas tardes, mi'jo.*"

Catalina jumped at the sound of the man's voice behind her, bidding her a good afternoon.

He'd called her a boy. That was good, right? That meant her disguise worked!

Like an animal caught unaware, she eased around to face him.

The man squinted and cocked his head at a funny angle. Recognition read on his surprised face. "*Eres mujer!*"

So much for the tiny victory. "Yes," Catalina whispered. "I'm a woman! Now please, go away."

She waited, expecting the man to respect her wishes, but he remained rooted to the spot.

"Since you are obviously new to town, I will explain to you why I can't do that." The man reached out a hand and introduced himself. "I am Father Emmanuel, and this is my parish."

Catalina frowned. Who was she supposed to trust in this town? Finally, she accepted the offered hand. "You don't look much like a priest."

Father Emmanuel glanced down at his rugged clothes then back to her, and chuckled. "You'll have to forgive me." He motioned for Catalina to follow him. He pointed at a window that overlooked the fenced-in grounds behind the church. A small wagon filled with numerous burlap bags stood on one side of a bountiful garden. "I was on a mission that required a more comfortable form of dress. In fact, I had just finished and was about to change back into my robes when I heard you come in."

The man paused, his gaze passing over Catalina in a respectful manner.

"So that is my excuse. Now what is yours?" Father Emmanuel pointed to Catalina's outlandish garb. "You don't look much like a woman."

Heat rushed to her cheeks and she dipped her head to hide her embarrassment.

"Oh, well." She shrugged. "The Bible says 'the truth shall set you free.' So I guess there's no place better to start than here with you."

Father Emmanuel cupped her elbow and guided her to a pew. He listened, leaning towards her, occasionally sliding an arm along the back of the pew while Catalina explained the highlights of the ordeal she had been subjected to – Ben's accidental death, the pending trial, Matthew's help to get her out of North Carolina... And the abduction.

"The last two weeks at Jericho have been the worst of my entire life," she concluded.

"Whew!" The priest let out a low whistle and settled against the back of the pew. "That's an incredible story. Unfortunately, the last bit sounds too true to think it's made up. Belmonte has been operating under the guise of a saloon for a long time. Everyone who lives here knows the truth, though. Jericho is the last place any decent woman would willingly stay."

Hope bloomed in her belly.

"Then you'll help me?" she asked, tugging at his arm.

The priest brandished an arm around the sanctuary. "How? What would you suggest I do to go against someone like Belmonte? Your story is not new. He has been operating this disgusting business of selling women for almost two years now. And the people here leave him alone because he spends money in their shops to put food on their tables... Not to mention the small army of men at his bidding to kill anyone who stands in his way."

Catalina wandered to the front window that faced the street. She spied a couple of saloon hands knocking on neighboring doors and forcing their way in. She ducked back out of sight.

"They're coming! Could you help me hide?" She implored, desperation dripping from her voice. "Just until the men leave."

The priest hustled to the window, shielding her from view and hung his head in silent prayer.

Terror mounted as Catalina waited for his response. Would he toss her back out on the street? She had no other options, nowhere to run.

The deafening silence surged into a roar, above the roiling of her stomach roiling and the knocking of her knees.

The priest popped his head up, as if struck with divine inspiration, his face serene. "Yes. Come," he said. "I can hide you. I know the perfect spot. But we must hurry!"

He grabbed Catalina by the arm, pulling her to follow him. Together, they ran to the back of the parish and sprang out the backdoor, bursting into the empty garden with such force that even the stubborn burro hitched to the wagon took notice. He stomped a hoof with irritation as the priest rushed to the wagon.

"Help me with this one," he demanded.

Catalina rushed to his side and lifted one end of the heavy bag.

"What's in here?" she asked.

"Beans in some of the bags. This one is *masa*." Father Emmanuel replied. "Flour – for the people to make tortillas."

"Yes, I know what it is." She should, as many hours as she had spent at Jericho, pressing the dough for the saloon's patrons to enjoy with their meals. "You're going to give this away to them?"

The priest bobbed his head. "I was going to." He pulled out a knife and cut open one end of it, then dumped the flour out onto the ground. Father Emmanuel shook the bag clean.

"What are you doing?" she asked.

"Helping you hide. Now climb up into the wagon and pull this over your head." He handed her the empty sack.

Taking off the sombrero, she did as she was told. She sat on the hat, allowing the sack to be pulled over her head. How surprising to see that she could fit inside completely. She shifted and stuffed the open end underneath her.

"Okay, I'm in." Despite the effort to remain calm, her voice shook. "How long do we have to wait?"

"We don't." The priest said as he piled other bags of *masa* and *frijoles* around her. "I was just thinking… That name you said earlier – Matthew – I met a man a few days ago with the same name. Maybe it is him. If it is, then I think I know where to find him."

Catalina sucked in a jagged breath.

Could it be true?

"You know where Matthew is?"

"Maybe yes, maybe no," the priest said, his voice muffled through the burlap.

The courtyard gate opened with a squeak. Then the sound of the priest's feet shuffling in the dirt stopped. He must have mounted the burro. "Now be very still. We're going to slip you right past these *banditos* and they'll never suspect a thing."

Catalina crouched down even lower, struggling to catch a fresh snatch of air.

"It's awfully stuffy in here," she complained.

"Shhh." The priest demanded silence. "They're right ahead."

Catalina forced her breathing to slow. What if she died in the wagon from suffocation? Better that than at the hands of El Perro or inside the walls of Jericho!

The cart moved forward, and Catalina closed her eyes with a prayer that their plan would work. She barely reached "amen" and the wagon stopped again.

"*Párate… A dónde vas?*"

El Perro! He demanded the priest's destination.

A shudder rippled through her body. Would he give away her whereabouts?

"*A los pobres.*" Father Emmanuel shifted on the wagon seat.

The smell of flour tickled Catalina's nose, and she stifled a sneeze. With dread coursing through her veins, she listened to the sound of gun clicks.

POP!

The sound of a bullet planting itself into a nearby bag almost made her scream.

"*Ya!*" One of the men yelled. "Stop wasting bullets."

"Okay," El Perro responded and the tearing of burlap could be heard.

He must be using a knife!

The sound of beans pouring out of a sack reached her ears. The process repeated. Another satchel torn; contents spilled. They would waste every ounce of food just to find her!

"*Hijo,*" Catalina listened when the priest spoke. "Why do you destroy the people's food? These bags are meant to feed the poor – the ones that Señor Francisco

Villa is fighting so hard to provide for. What if he were to learn of this waste?"

Father Emmanuel paused and allowed the men to consider his words. It didn't take much for them to realize that destroying the bags of food would be viewed as an attack on the Mexican people.

An act that Pancho Villa would never forgive.

With the distaste of murdering a priest on their tongues, the men motioned for Father Emmanuel to move along.

The wagon lurched forward, and Catalina almost gasped out loud. She clamped her forearm over her mouth.

The stubborn burro returned to his sluggish pace, his heels clomping against the road.

Catalina poached inside the thick brown cloth. Beads of sweat moistened her hairline and ran down her cheeks. She resisted the urge to wipe them away, the rhythmic jostling of the wagon wheels putting her in a semi trance. Or was she close to swoon from the blistering heat? Would she jeopardize her whereabouts if she called out to the priest? Were there any witnesses around? The only thing she could be certain of was that she would faint without fresh air.

She reached up and determinedly worked her slender fingers through soggy curls – one pulling loose as she yanked out a hairpin.

"Sorry, Father Emmanuel," she whispered under her breath before jabbing the pin into the side of the burlap. Any hope of its future use was destroyed as the pin successfully pierced the bag. Then she worked two fingers through the hole, creating a gap large enough to such a lungful of air.

Focused on the task of simply breathing, Catalina lost track of the time. How long had they ridden? The unbearable heat that made her feel like the ride would never end, but the jostling wasn't as fierce as before.

Was the wagon slowing down?

Yes!

The priest called out a greeting as the wheels ground to a halt. Weight lifted from the wagon, and footsteps pounded the dirt next to the cart

"Does this look like anyone you know?" The padre pulled the burlap sack off her head.

Precious air! Catalina lifted her face to the sun and gulped in a lungful. Rejuvenated, she peered out from behind wild, sweaty curls.

"Matthew!"

Hardly able to corral her excitement, she jumped up. The sombrero she had sat on wrapped around the oversized boots and she lost all balance. Arms flailing, she fell.

Matthew raced forward and held out his arms to steady her, wincing slightly from the pain in his shoulder.

His hands circled her waist and lifted her off the wagon. Then he planted her firmly on the ground. Releasing only one hand to brush away a few flyaway strands of her limp curls, he smiled.

Was she dreaming? She stared up at him, taking in every line of his face. He had tanned a bit, but otherwise looked the same as always. She smiled at him, knees buckling when he finally spoke.

"Catalina," he whispered, her name like a precious jewel on his tongue.

Then he eased forward.

Chapter Twenty

"Eh hem," a throat cleared.

Catalina tore her gaze away from Matthew to glance at the woman who stood with her arms crossed around her thick body, red-hot anger clearly etched into her face.

"You must be the one my Matthew has been talking about." Head held high, she addressed Catalina as though speaking to a useless servant.

"*Your* Matthew?" Catalina bristled at the woman's superior tone.

"Now see here, Amorina—" Matthew interrupted.

Father Emmanuel stepped forward and laid a hand on Matthew's shoulder. "Perhaps it would be best if we all went inside before this goes any further."

"Yes," The woman named Amorina agreed, cocking a wicked brow at Catalina. "I don't know where you're from, but we Mexicans have enough manners to greet our hosts and their families upon arrival."

Catalina huffed, the ride in the stuffy bag and the shock of seeing Matthew draining the last of her strength, but of all the nerve! As if she wasn't a proper lady because she didn't offer her name. *Well, excuse me!* She planted fists on her denim-clad hips, but the stance was lost beneath the poncho. "Why, I never!"

She was about to give the forward hostess a piece of her own mind, but Matthew headed her off.

"Come, Catalina. Let's go inside. You can cool off. I will pour you a tall glass of water." He motioned to the hacienda that stood before them.

Cool air? Water? Catalina conceded and glanced at the ranch for the first time. The ghostly remains of a once-grand home, the royal exterior now a faded blue dress, the worn *teja* roof pale and missing some of her auburn tresses. The ones that remained broke off into split ends. Age and filth had clouded the windows like dreaded cataracts, and the door hung haphazardly like a crooked tooth in an old face.

An unintended shiver crept down Catalina's spine, causing the hair on her arm to stand on end, despite the insufferable heat. She shook off the feeling as everyone followed Amorina into the house.

"Papa!" The woman called her father as soon as they stepped into a humble receiving room, simply decorated with several pillowed rocking chairs. She gestured for them to sit.

They gathered around a small round table of smooth oak, a knotted knee in one lonely leg.

"Papa! *Donde estás*? We have visitors. Father Emmanuel *y una cualquiera*."

Catalina darkened with embarrassment of being linked to Jericho. Dressed in men's clothing, she didn't think anyone – least of all another woman – would guess that she had spent any time entertaining men. She suddenly felt silly in her ridiculous disguise, but the feeling was quickly swept away when an elderly man hobbled into the room.

"Papa! What happened?" Amorina rushed over to her father and tried to take his arm, but the elderly man shooed her away.

"*Estoy bien*! I only had a little trouble with that green horse." Her father limped towards one of the chairs and sat down with a low groan. He wiped the back of his hand across his sweaty brow, and focused on his company. "*Disculpa*. I'm so sorry for not receiving you better, but I didn't expect company. Please, please sit down."

A flick of the hand sent Amorina scurrying away for refreshments. The belittling action left an uncomfortable silence.

Father Emanuel covered it up with ease. "Buenos días, Juan. It's good to see you're doing well."

Juan waved off the comment. "Believe me, Father, I feel much worse than I look." He patted his knees in an effort to indicate an old complaint. "Every bit of me aches so much that I can hardly work the earth anymore. In fact, I wouldn't have planted my field this year if it hadn't been for my future son-in-law."

The old man smiled at Matthew.

Catalina gasped, her hand fluttering to her heart. What? Future son-in-law? She looked between the two men, trying to hide the despair from eking out on her face.

"So it's true," she whispered. "You really are promised to someone else."

Juan shook his head affirmatively. "That's righ—"

"Now wait a minute," Matthew interrupted their host. He waved off the idea, addressing Catalina more so than the old man. "I don't know what you've heard, but I can guarantee you it isn't true. I am not now – nor will I ever be – engaged to Miss Rangel."

Juan Rangel clucked his tongue in irritation.

"What's this?" He acted indignant. "You string along my daughter only to toss her aside the moment you see some ugly face? Look at her! Dressed like a man – a dirty drifter, no less. I will not have it, young man! You made a promise to my daughter… a promise that you will keep by your own integrity, or at the end of my shotgun."

Matthew bristled at the old man's threat, bolting to his feet with fists at his side.

The priest stood as well, taking swift command of the scene by placing a hand on Matthew's shoulder.

"Don Rangel," Father Emmanuel formally addressed the man, but his voice was bold. "You tread a sinful path and you know it."

All three men stared at one another, the dead air stiffening in the silence. Suddenly, Juan hung his head as though ashamed to have been caught in a lie.

"You can't blame me for trying." He released a defeated sigh and plunked back down in the chair, motioning for Matthew to do the same. "Relax. You're not the first man that my daughter has latched onto."

"It's true," Father Emmanuel confirmed as they all took their seats again. "You're the fourth man in eight months to step inside my church without the slightest idea of proposing to her."

"Then why did you try to pretend otherwise?" Matthew questioned Juan.

The old man shrugged in response. "I hoped it was true this time," he began. "Things have been so much easier with you around here. Your help on the ranch has made all the difference. Fields planted, horses broke in. And then there's the improvement in my daughter's demeanor. Honestly, I haven't seen Amorina this happy in almost two years." He hung his head. "Since her mother passed on."

"Oh, I'm so sorry for your loss." Catalina said, empathy squeezing the words from her mouth.

"Thank you. You're very kind," Juan replied. "And I'm guessing you somehow know him?" He motioned to Matthew.

"I thought I did."

Matthew took his hat off and slapped it against his knee, shooting her with an incredulous look. "Now what's that supposed to mean? Of course we know each other! We spent days on the road together."

"Oh, really?" Catalina crossed her arms over her chest and glared back at him. "Then why did you ignore me when you were in town? And don't lie! I'd know that ugly hat anywhere. You were climbing into a wagon with her." Catalina gestured at Amorina as she reentered the room, setting a tray of café con leche and pan on the table.

The woman glanced up, and caught everyone's stare. A small, antagonizing smile formed as she pushed the tray closer to Matthew, offering him the coffee and sweet pastries. "He and I needed to speak with Father Emmanuel about some personal business." She cast an adoring glance at Matthew.

"Amorina," Juan gave his daughter a look of warning. "I already know the truth. So don't make things any harder than what they have to be."

The woman studied her father before glancing over to their guests. Her gaze rested on Matthew, as if weighing his response to an unspoken question. The answer was painted in his hard-set eyes. Pursing her thin lips, Amorina excused herself and slipped out of the room, her back rigid and head held proud.

Matthew waited until the trail end of her dress disappeared then ran a free hand through his hair before giving his head a shake.

The small habit wasn't lost on Catalina.

"Look here, Cat. I know what you think you saw, but you've got it all wrong." Matthew explained everything that had happened since the moment the two of them had been attacked back in Texas, to the day she had called out to him from the saloon courtyard.

Catalina raised a quizzical brow.

Father Emmanuel must've seen her doubtful expression and rushed to support Matthew's claim. "It's true, Señorita."

"Sí, es verdad." Juan chimed in. "I know it sounds like a tall tale, but I watched my daughter nurse him back to health." The elderly gent smiled at Matthew, something sad and wistful, fatherly. "I suppose that is one of the reasons she attached to you so quickly. And I'm sorry I tried to take advantage of the situation."

The old man stood to apologize.

Standing to accept it, Matthew took a firm hold of the outstretched hand and gave it a good shake before turning back to Catalina.

"I hope you believe me when I say that I honestly didn't mean to hurt you. I could never abandon you like that." He crossed the room to where she sat and knelt in front of her, lightly taking her hands in his. "Catalina, I don't mind admitting that I nearly broke down when I remembered what had happened and realized it was you behind that gate. Right then, I was determined to get you back no matter what it took. I knew I could never do it alone, though. So I prayed for God's help. I don't ever recall praying so hard in my life, wondering if God would even hear me. But He did and here you are –

proof that miracles really do happen. Now I'm praying for another miracle – one where you say you'll give me another chance."

The sincerity in his voice brought tears to her eyes.

His eyes were bright with hope, and she could see the change in him.

She broke out in a broad smile. "You prayed for me?"

Matthew produced a smile equal to hers. He let out an exasperated sigh, but judging by the playful gleam flashing from his eyes, she suspected it was fake.

"Well, I'm a Christian," he explained. "It's what we do. Right?"

"Oh, Matthew!" Catalina threw her arms around his neck, embracing him with such enthusiasm that they toppled backwards onto the floor.

Catalina unlocked her arms from around his neck and rolled off of him, ready to apologize, but his eyes, full of mirth and joy, stopped her.

He let out a throaty laugh and the priest and Juan joined in.

When he stopped laughing, Matthew stood and extended a hand to help her up.

Catalina brushed herself off and cleared her throat.

"Eh hem, well." She tried to find something to say.

Matthew jumped in to her rescue. Again. "So, I guess we should try to resume our original mission." Matthew suggested. "That is, if you feel you'll be safe there?"

Catalina hesitated. "There were other women like me at Jericho. And children! Oh, Matthew. It was horrible! I keep wondering if there's anything I can do to help them.

Matthew sighed.

"I know you want to help them, and its right to feel that way. I just don't think we can, though. Not right now when there's obviously someone out to harm you. Truthfully? I don't even think it's safe for you to be in Mexico, but I keep thinking we can't go back either."

Catalina thought for a moment.

"You're right. I don't think Mexico is safe anymore, either. However, I feel like I'll be safer here than back in Charlotte. At least, for right now. I mean, our problems began while we were still in the States. So how much safer am I going to be there?"

"That's what I was thinking," Matthew agreed. "Whoever attacked us before we could cross the border had already been following us for a while. So it would probably be wiser to find your family here. They could possibly provide a safe haven while we try to figure out whom we're dealing with. The problem will be getting there."

"That's true. We don't know exactly where we're going – not to mention that we don't even have a way to get there."

"Maybe I can help." Juan spoke up. "I've lived in this area all my life."

Matthew turned to Juan, hope brightening his eyes. "Have you heard of the Santiago family from Maravatío?"

"Of course," their host stated. "Miguel Santiago is one of my cousins. His ranch lies a couple of days from here. It's hard riding, though."

Matthew tapped his forehead. "I knew I recognized your name. You're related to Cat's family."

This man and his daughter were family? Stunned, Catalina turned to the old man. "We're related? "Then you know my father, Gian... I mean, Carlos Santiago?"

"The only Carlos Santiago I ever knew was Miguel's son," Juan said. "But he left Mexico a long time ago when he was barely a man. If I remember correctly, he left after an argument with his father. That's the last anyone heard of him… or your sister. Isn't that right?" Juan addressed the priest.

A grave look fell over Father Emmanuel's face.

"Yes," he replied, his gaze skimming Catalina with hope and longing burning from his eyes. "Our parents died in an accident shortly after I joined the church. So I took charge of my sister. She was in love with Carlos, but I thought her too young to marry. So I forbade it. She was a very headstrong girl, though. She ran off with him anyway." He shook his head, a heavy sigh escaping as he hung his head. "It was the last I ever saw of her."

So that would make the padre her—

"You mean you had no idea that she had crossed into America," Matthew questioned Father Emmanuel, "or that she had a family of her own?"

Uncle. Her jaw dropped, the news buckling her knees.

Matthew grabbed hold of her elbow, saving her from puddling on the floor.

"No," Father Emmanuel admitted. He raised his hands, but his steps faltered and he dropped them back to his side. His face grew serious. "I'm sorry, young lady. I just can't imagine you belong to my sister. It is too much of a coincidence. You must look like your father."

"Not at all." The rejection hit Catalina hard. "I look exactly like my mother. That is, when I'm not dressed like this." Catalina swept a hand along her frame.

All heads angled towards her ghastly clothes.

"That is a bit of a problem," Matthew said. A corner of his mouth lifted in jest. "We'll need to find you some suitable clothes before we can press on. After all, I couldn't possibly deliver you to your grandfather looking like some boy plucked out of a herding posse."

Catalina placed her hands on her hips, ready to fire off a witty reply but Amorina walked back into the room to clear the table.

"You may borrow one of my daughter's dresses," he stated.

Amorina jerked up with a loud gasp, almost dropping the tray.

Juan ignored his daughter's dramatics and continued speaking. "She has several of her own, as well as the ones she inherited from her mother. Besides, you two are family."

Horror played across the woman's face.

She stepped forward, pressed a gentle hand on Amorina's arm. "We just discovered that we're cousins of sorts. I mean, we are a bit removed. Nonetheless, we're related if I'm not mistaken." Her attempt at pleasant conversation rambled, and Amorina's face glazed. "In fact, it would appear that we're all related in some way. Well, all of us except Matthew, I guess."

Matthew came to stand beside Catalina. He placed a protective arm around her back, and looked down at her.

"I aim to change that soon enough," he assured.

A tender, safe feeling settled into Catalina's chest.

Matthew's eyes glowed with love and promise – a promise she could stake her life on.

As if she hadn't already.

In that moment, when all else faded into the background, and it was just her and him gazing into each other's faces, Catalina knew beyond a shadow of doubt that Matthew was the one for her.

Thank You, God, for choosing such a wonderful man for my future! She snuggled closer to Matthew, allowing his reassuring arms to warm her.

The moment was short lived.

A strong tug yanked her out of Matthew's arms. Amorina?

Anger replaced her initial surprise. "What—"

"Come, *prima*." Her cousin smiled, a picture of mock innocence expertly painted on her face. "We must get you out of that frightful outfit and into something more fitting for a lady of your status."

Catalina eyed her newfound cousin with suspicion. The words were sweet, but they carried a weight of malice. Hesitant to follow her, Catalina replied.

"That's very kind of you, but I wouldn't want to ruin one of your beautiful dresses." She held her sooty hands up in explanation. "I'm afraid I've gotten a bit dirty along the way."

Amorina waved off the refusal. "Oh, that's easy to fix. You can bathe in the *manantial*. It isn't far from here."

"Yes," Juan nodded at his daughter. "That is a very good idea. It will give you the chance to clean up before continuing on your journey, as well as time for the two of you to get to know each other better."

Amorina smiled back at her father. "Yes," she agreed. "We will be better than cousins. We will be like sisters!"

Catalina bit her lower lip, ashamed for thinking the worst of Amorina. That the girl had it out for her when, in reality, the poor girl was probably trying to deal with the fact that Matthew wasn't in love with her.

Like how hurt and angry she had been when Benjamin informed her that he would marry a Harrington instead of her.

Had Matthew treated Amorina the same as Ben had treated her? Had there been empty promises and stolen kisses?

She glanced up at Matthew and immediately knew the answer. He wasn't the sort to toy with a woman's affections. Still, Catalina empathized with her cousin and appreciated that Amorina chose to be gracious, despite her unrequited love.

"All right," Catalina finally spoke. "Let's go to this *manantial* you mentioned. I'd love to feel like myself again!"

The woman latched onto her arm.

"Wait a minute," Father Emmanuel halted their progress. "The spring Amorina mentioned is a dangerous one called *La Bruja*."

"The Witch?" Matthew questioned. He eyed Amorina, suspicion darkening his face. "Why is it called that?"

"Because it has a natural *remolino*," Amorina replied with a casual lift of one shoulder.

"Absolutely not." Matthew shook his head as he addressed Catalina. "After everything we've been through, there is no way I'm letting you near a whirlpool."

"A whirlpool!" Catalina exclaimed. She looked back at Amorina, trying to gauge her cousin's intentions.

The woman's face read complete calm. Was she trustworthy?

Juan Rangel cleared his throat.

"It's true," he said. "*La Bruja* does have a whirlpool, but it is still very safe. Why, I myself have gone swimming in it many times. Besides, you will not have to go in very far just to bathe."

"That's right," Amorina chimed in. "You could just wade in maybe waist deep. And it would be much faster than gathering kindling and heating up water for a bath."

Catalina considered the idea and warmed up to it. A bath sounded divine. The quicker, the better. "She's right, Matthew. If I'm fast about it, then we can get back on the road today. We could reach my grandfather's ranch before anyone even makes our tracks."

Matthew rubbed the back of his neck with one of his hands. Uncertainty clouded his expression. "I don't know. I understand you want to look proper-like the first time you see your grandfather, but I'm used to trusting my instincts and something about this just doesn't feel right. Maybe I should go with you."

Catalina gave her head a firm shake.

"She's right," Amorina spoke. "It would look bad if someone were to ride by and see you there while she was bathing. Besides, I will be with her."

"As will I," Father Emmanuel volunteered. "I'm well-regarded with all the neighbors in the area. So no one would question my intentions should they see me there." He smiled at Catalina. "Besides, as my niece, it is my responsibility and privilege to keep watch over you."

Catalina swung her gaze to Matthew to gauge his opinion.

He nodded his agreement with the plan.

She turned back to Father Emmanuel. Her uncle. A swell of affection washed over her. "All right then. Thank you." She agreed before addressing Amorina. "You sure you don't mind me borrowing one of your dresses?"

"Not at all," Amorina exclaimed as she led Catalina out of the sitting room and down a short, dimly lit corridor. The only light visible came from the crack of a bedroom door. Amorina pushed the door, the heavy wood creaking.

Light streamed from the long windows, nearly blinding Catalina.

As her eyes adjusted to the light, Amorina went to her wardrobe and plucked out a couple of dresses.

"I have these two here," she said. "They aren't the very best, but they certainly aren't the worst."

Catalina fingered the calico fabric on one of the dresses. Pretty, but certainly nothing like she had worn back home. Not that those fancy dresses with their matching purses and ribbons mattered anymore. How could she care about such frivolous possessions now that she knew there were women and children being abused in abominable ways?

But she couldn't think about that now. She could only fight one battle at a time, and that meant staying alive if she wanted to help the others later. She held the dress up, inspecting it.

"On the contrary," she replied, "I think they're beautiful. Thank you for letting me borrow one."

Amorina waved her off. "Don't worry about it. Just pick one and let's go."

Catalina plucked up the calico dress with a giggle. "You seem even more eager than I am to get to that swimming hole."

"Well, it's very beautiful." Amorina closed her eyes and lifted her face as if she were there, on the beach, the water cooling her toes. Her eyelids fluttered open, and she snapped back. She scooped up the second dress and hung it in the closet. "So I try swimming in it every chance I get. That's all."

"And is it really as dangerous as Matthew feared?"

Did Amorina wince at the mention of Matthew's name? Poor girl. She must have it bad

"Not at all. In fact, I've swum in the *remolino* itself."

"Really?" Catalina asked, awestruck at the idea of her cousin attempting something so bold. "I've never even seen a whirlpool, let alone swam in one. You must have been really scared the first time."

"*Claro que no*," Amorina shook her head. "The one in our spring is very weak. Why, a small child could easily swim through it."

"Well, why did Father Emmanuel seem so concerned if it's as gentle as you say?" Catalina questioned.

Amorina gave Catalina a patronizing smile, as though a small child had asked her a question with such an obvious answer.

"Because he is from the town – not *el rancho*. He doesn't even know what it would be like to take a dip in our spring."

"So there isn't any danger at all?" Catalina persisted. "No one has ever drowned swimming in it?"

"I can only speak on one account. From before my time and the reason that the spring earned its name *La Bruja*."

"What happened?" Catalina sat on the edge of Amorina's bed and listened to the woman weave her tail.

"Once upon a time… too long for me to really know when… there was a beautiful peasant girl who lived a few ranches away from the *manantial*. She would walk there sometimes, passing the other farm houses, just to gather water. As she walked, she sang a sweet, wishful tune for true love. One day, the tune found the ear of a farm boy. Mesmerized by her beauty, he decided to try to win her hand. He brought her rare wildflowers and sweet pan. Still, the girl's father would not consent to their marriage. He knew his daughter's beauty could fetch a large dowry. So he promised her to an old, rich *ejido* landowner instead. Hearing of the arrangement, the girl fell into a horrible state of depression. But the father was moved only by greed, and would not change his mind. So on the day before the fateful wedding, the young woman went on one last walk to gather water, stopping at the farm boy's house to say her goodbyes. However, the only person home was the young man's mother, who informed the girl that her son had left home two days prior… determined to find his fortune so that he wouldn't be turned away the next time he found love. Saddened to hear that the farm boy was already looking for another, the bride-to-be made her way to the *manantial*."

Amorina paused for a moment, a wicked gleam in her eyes. She turned to her cousin.

"Do you know what she did then?"

Entranced, Catalina shook her head.

"They say… she threw herself in and drowned!" Catalina gasped. Satisfied, Amorina smiled. "Only it wasn't because the boy had run off to find fortune and love. Having no intention of killing herself over a man, the girl decided to gather the water and go home. She'd marry the *ejido* and learn to love him, despite his many wrinkles and foul breath. That is, until she got to the *manantial*. There beside the water, she found a large clay jug. And out in the water, floating round and round the *remolino*, was the young man. Apparently, he had gone to the lake to drink away his sorrows. He didn't mean to drown," Amorina finished the tale. "He was just too *borracho* to swim after falling into the lake."

Catalina shuddered at the word *borracho*. It was how the ladies at Jericho described the men when they stumbled out of the saloon after a night of festivities.

"But what about the girl?" She asked.

"Well, she couldn't just leave him there." Amorina shrugged. "After all, he kind of died because of her. So she tried to fish him out, but was weighed down by her clothes and drowned, too."

Catalina groaned. What a sad fate for such a young couple!

"But we don't have to worry about that." Amorina tugged on her arm to leave.

A sense of uneasiness settled in the pit of Catalina's stomach. Still she followed her hostess out of the room, clutching the calico dress as though it were kin to salvation.

Chapter Twenty-One

The wagon jostled back and forth. The scenery passed by at a snail's pace. The greenery here was sparse compared to the countryside back home. The trees looked like thick bodies with long, gnarled fingers shooting out of them. Their leaves were prickly-looking like cactus, casting off a hostile air.

"What funny little trees," Catalina finally remarked.

Amorina followed her gaze. She shook her head in disagreement. "Not funny. That is the Yucca and they are amazing," she explained. "You are just not seeing them when they are in full bloom. During the spring, each one will fill with big, beautiful flowers."

"That's something I'd like to see," Catalina replied before turning back to study the trees once more. Without the flowers, they looked like hands reaching up to the sky.

Much like the tree dubbed "Joshua" that she had studied in her college history class. Staring at the crooked branches, Catalina could imagine a man reaching his hands towards the heavens, praying for God to make the sun stand still. Eyes closed, she tilted her face upward and allowed the day's warmth to caress her skin. She let out a peaceful sigh.

It was going to be a wonderful day.

"*Ya, ya.*" Father Emmanuel snapped the reins against the horse.

Catalina's eyes popped open.

They had hardly spoken during the ride, and she could only guess that he was still trying to process the information of them being related to one another. He'd made a joke about everyone in the pueblo being related, then had fallen into silence, focusing on driving the horse down the dirt path to the cool spring ahead.

The wagon slowed at the bottom of a hill. The worn dirt path abruptly ended before a lush patch of green grass took over. A meager smattering of wildflowers dotted the ground, growing denser as the hill rose.

Catalina slid out of the wagon and collected the borrowed toiletries.

"It's just a small climb to the *manantial*," Father Emmanuel pointed to the top of the hill. "Amorina will escort you while I wait here and keep a watch over the area."

"Thank you," Catalina said, waiting until his gaze connected with hers. She smiled, then followed Amorina through the blanket of yellow, white and purple flowers that kissed her ankles. Their delicious fragrance wafted up to her. They reached the peak of the hill and she surveyed the landscape.

"It's beautiful," she exclaimed as she came upon the sight of the large spring-fed pond beneath long, weepy trees. Their branches lightly swayed in the wind before reaching down towards the water, their end leaves making ripples that gradually swelled outward until finally disappearing.

Catalina skimmed the length of the *manantial*, her eyes landing on the far end where the water circled round and around. It reminded her of when she was younger and would play with her sweet tea at the dinner table. She would use her spoon to swirl the drink until a tiny hurricane would appear. Would the *remolino* resemble a hurricane under the water?

"See how far away it is?" Amorina asked. "You have nothing to worry about. So go on. I will hang your dress up for you on that tree over there."

Catalina's gaze followed to where Amorina pointed, to the other side of the pond – a mere five feet away from the *remolino*.

"Why that one?" she questioned. Uneasiness slithered into the pit of her stomach.

"Because it's the only one with a branch low enough to reach," Amorina responded before adding, "And you certainly can't leave it on the ground. Right?"

"It doesn't—"

Amorina cut her off. "Exactly." She waved Catalina away. "That's why I'm going to hang it over there. Then I'll walk back up the hill to help keep watch."

Catalina let out a slow, anxious sigh as she made her way towards the pond. She hesitated only a moment before undressing. Then she edged towards the water, allowing one bare foot to test its coolness.

"Oh, that's nice." Catalina murmured as warmth drifted up to cover her ankles. She leaned back to wet her hair and soon, she was immersed to her neck, humming as she worked the rose-scented soap into a rich lather, determined to scrub the roadside dust from each limp curl.

She rinsed, luxuriating in the silky feel of the water as it rippled across her bare skin. Like a toddler playing in a tub, she flipped over and flopped her arms out to her side, the past few weeks of trauma sliding off her back.

She stayed like that until wrinkles crinkled her fingers. She climbed out of the *manantial,* squeezed the water from her hair then fetched her clothes. Once she finished dressing, she turned back to the *remolino,* mesmerized by the circling motion. The soapy grime from her body floated towards it, and now followed the downward spiral. Catalina found herself entranced by the soothing, steady flow of water.

A loud crack shattered the moment of tranquility.

What? Catalina whipped her head around to stare at the splintered tree, one branch drooping from the trunk.

Another crack forced Catalina to jump back.

The heel of her shoe caught a gnarled root from the old tree, and she tumbled backwards, arms flailing wildly around her, nothing but thin air to latch onto. She squealed, but the water swallowed her scream. She bounced back up, but the swift undercurrent snatched up the hem of her dress. In an instant, the strong tug of water dragged her into the *remolino.*

She was going to drown! Fear propelled her into action, her arms pumping against the current, but her legs tangled in her undergarments. The weight of her wet clothes started to drag her under. She took a deep breath right before her head submerged. She kicked and resurfaced, but her strength faded with every stroke.

"Catalina!" Matthew?

She raised her head in the direction of the voice.

Matthew dangled from a low branch of the splintered tree, one arm wrapped around a spindly branch, the other waving.

Her Matthew. He'd found her.

She dipped under the water once again.

Was he too late?

Matthew wormed his way down the too-thin branch, gritting his teeth when a large splinter bit into his palm. He swallowed a swear, calling out for God's grace instead. The idea that he wasn't doing this alone fortified him, and he ignored the fire that burned his raw hands. He continued his shaky crawl down the slick branch.

It bowed under his weight.

"Cat," he yelled, tightening his legs around the limb. He leaned down towards her, using the weakening tree as an anchor for one arm as he stretched the other. "Grab a hold of me!"

She reached up for his hand, missing it by a fraction before she squeaked out a weak "I can't." Her head bobbed under again.

"Catalina!" Matthew yelled again, desperation making him drop the other arm. The branch bent dangerously low as he hung upside down, mere inches away from the water's surface, foam from the swirl spraying into his nose.

The instant she re-emerged, he grabbed the cuff of her collar. He tugged and held on. Now what? Upside down, he had no leverage.

"Grab my belt."

Exhaustion etched her wet face, and defeat shadowed her eyes. Her mouth opened, but nothing came out.

He wouldn't let her give up! "Come on, hon, you can do it."

Wood crackled underneath this legs.

He froze. Catalina's eyes widened with fright.

He didn't dare move. "Don't worry," he soothed. "We'll make it, but I need you to do exactly what I say. Okay?"

He was rewarded with a terse nod.

"Good girl. I'm going to pull you up just a little more," he explained. "Just enough for you to reach up and grab a hold of the branch."

"I can't," Catalina sobbed.

"Yes, you can." Matthew reassured her. "I know you're tired, darling, but it'll only be for a split second. Okay?"

She panted out a small "okay" before feeling her weak body being tugged upward. Matthew swung her toward the branch as it gave another splintering cry from under him. Catalina wrapped her limp arms around the sound part of the limb on the opposite side of the break. She brought her legs up to wrap them around the branch and began to shinny along it. Matthew reached out and followed behind her.

"Oh," she cried, stopping.

"You're almost there," Matthew urged her from behind. "You can do this. Keep going. Come on, honey."

Matthew's spurring worked.

Catalina continued her crawl until she hung over the bank of the *manantial*, and slowly unwrapped her legs.

Matthew dropped down to the earth below and reached up for her.

Catalina released the tree from her death-like grip, and landed in his arms.

Exhausted, Matthew crumbled under Catalina and they both fell to the ground. He let out a loud grunt.

"Sorry." Catalina rolled off of him, laying on her back, panting.

She fit just right snug against the crook in his arm, her palm flat against his chest. He didn't plan to ever let her go.

She pushed back clumps of wet hair, her voice throaty and hoarse. "What happened? Everything was so peaceful. I was looking down at the water and then I thought I heard a shot."

"You did." Matthew confirmed her suspicions. "Amorina took a potshot at you."

"What?" Catalina angled her face towards him. "How did she manage that? Father Em— um, my uncle would have seen her."

Matthew rolled onto his side, rested his chin in his sore palm, elbow on the ground.

"She used the butt of a gun to cold cock him before shooting at you."

Catalina gasped and a tremor shook her body.

With his free hand, he gave her arm a brisk rub. She was so cold. "Don't worry. He'll be alright."

"Thank God," Catalina whispered.

"Yes," Matthew replied. "And thanks to Him that Amorina isn't much of a shot. The belly gun she was carrying was made for short distance, but long range shots can still cause some serious damage."

"I can't believe my cousin tried to shoot me." The shattered tree drew Catalina's gaze. She shuddered. "You're my hero. Again." She looked up, thankful.

He wanted to be that man for her. Always.

"Where did you leave Amorina?"

"Hogtied in the back of the wagon." He gave her a mischievous grin before lightly wrapping his free arm around her.

"Now I could get used to this," he said.

Catalina let out a small giggle, and he inhaled the clean, wet smell of her hair. His lungs filled with mint and he smiled.

"I think I prefer the smell of mint to that sweaty, masa fragrance you were wearing earlier."

"You're wicked," she joked. But her shoulders relaxed into his embrace.

Matthew lightly massaged her arm, slowly erasing the anxiety she had just felt. Catalina let out a deep sigh. "Although, that does feel quite wonderful."

Catalina looked up and found herself gazing into his stormy eyes. The uncertainty she had felt at the beginning of their journey no longer existed. She no longer questioned if she deserved to be loved. A sense of peace caressed her heart and she knew that God's perfect will included the man who stared back at her, adoration etched into the creases of his familiar face.

"Matthew—"

"Catalina—"

They both began and stopped.

Matthew chuckled. The weight of this delicate, yet spitfire of a woman in his arms sobered him. He tightened his grip around her. If only he could keep her safe forever.

"What am I going to do with you, darling?" Matthew sighed and kissed the top of her head.

A low feminine growl pierced the peace and then, "Get away from my husband!"

Catalina jerked against him at the sound of Amorina's voice. Both she and Matthew jumped up.

"I would hardly call you his wife," she exclaimed as she tried to confront the woman. However, Matthew held her back, continuing to shield her from Amorina.

"Maybe not yet, but he will be once you're out of the way." She pointed the same gun with expert aim at Catalina's head. "I doubt I'll miss this time."

Matthew took a step forward. *How in the world?* The woman was like a bad toothache. "I tied that rope pretty tight. How were you able to escape?"

"What? You thought I'd carry a gun, but not a knife?" Amorina snorted, something ugly and vindictive. "*Ay, amor.* You have a lot to learn about how life really is in Mexico."

"And you have a lot to learn about life in general," Catalina shot from behind. "You can't make someone love you. Trust me when I say it doesn't end well."

"She's right," Matthew agreed, putting out an arm to slide her behind him again, but she refused to budge. "We've already talked about this, and you know how I feel. Killing Catalina isn't going to make me love you. If anything, it'll make me resent you even more than I do right now."

Amorina's face crumbled.

"You resent me?"

Matthew let out a heavy sigh. His years of experience studying criminals had alerted him to the idea that Amorina might need medical attention.

Appeasing the woman and staying on her good side apparently hadn't worked. Physically exhausted and mentally drained, anger swelled, but he didn't punch it back down this time. Instead, he handed it over to God.

Please, Lord. I need to stay calm. Take away this anger, and fill me with Your peace.

"How can I not?" Matthew swallowed. His gaze stayed on the weapon in Amorina's hand, but he took in their surroundings. What could he use against her? "Look at what you're doing. You're pointing a gun at the woman I love, threatening to kill her. Would you feel very kindly if you were in my position? What if someone was threatening to shoot me?"

His words appeared to resonate with the woman. The gun slowly began to lower.

Matthew lurched forward and grabbed it. He latched onto Amorina's wrist.

"Let's go." He escorted the defeated woman back to the wagon, Catalina following at a safe distance on the opposite side of her cousin.

"I'm impressed," she leaned in and whispered. "I was praying you'd know what to say to make her change her mind."

"So was I," Matthew admitted. "It's nice to know you were, too."

He rewarded her with a quick wink as they trudged up the hill towards the wagon, the warm sun beating down on their backs. He hoped Father Emmanuel was all right, and able to help hold Amorina down so the ropes would be *extra* tight this time.

Catalina's cried out. The sharp sound alerted Matthew.

He looked up to see half a dozen men standing along the crest. The sun glared off the rifles pointed down at them.

Amorina began to laugh.

He glanced sideways at the woman. Had she lost her mind?

Catalina's head shook, her face a mask of horror. Shock?

He couldn't deal with that now. He jerked Amorina's wrists.

"What?" She smirked as if she had the final say. "Did you think I'd just hand over the only weapon I had without some sort of plan? I didn't really have a knife. Those rouges happened by and agreed to let me go. All I had to do was get you two back up the hill. Nobody wanted to risk coming down near the *remolino*."

Matthew squinted up at the group of *banditos*. One, two… five, six… He rubbed the spot where the bullet had grazed his head.

"Hey, I remember you." He gritted at one of the men, recognizing him from the Texas shootout.

"Yeah, I remember you too," the man snarled with a thick accent. "You got lucky the last time because you had your sheriff friend, but now you're alone."

He raised his rifle at Matthew.

"No," Catalina yelled and jumped in front of him.

Matthew shoved Amorina out of the way and grabbed Catalina by the waist and pivoted to set her behind him.

Another man rushed forward and grabbed Catalina by the arm, yanking her away from Matthew. "You've caused enough trouble, *estupida*." He bared his teeth at her. "My cousin is dead because of your little escape!"

The man raised his other hand and brought the backside of it down across her face, the smack echoing across the hill.

Catalina's head wobbled, her hand covering the cheek, already turning tomato red.

"Let go of her!" Matthew shouted and lunged at the man.

Two others jumped forward and grabbed an arm on either side, pulling him back from his attack.

The gunman turned, flipped his rifle over, and rammed the butt of it into Matthew's ribs.

Matthew doubled over, panting to catch a breath.

The leader of the pack cleared the crest. "That's enough!" he ordered, nodding his head at Catalina. "We're being paid to bring that one back alive. We'll bring the others and let Belmonte decide what he wants to do with them."

"Jericho?" Catalina whispered. She wagged her head, slow at first then a vicious shake, her cheek already swollen and purple. "No!" She tugged at her captor, but the man only moved to curl an arm around her waist.

"What do you mean by that?" Amorina shrunk back as one of the men approached her and took hold of her arm. "We had a deal!" She screamed.

The man lifted Catalina's wayward cousin up over a shoulder, laughing as her small fists pounded against his back. When one of her hands found a fistful of hair, he yelped and set her down long enough to slap her into compliance, then hauled her away.

Jericho.

The prison.

Catalina's head jerked towards Matthew, but he didn't dare glance at her. He couldn't, or they would have no chance of survival because he'd die trying to save her from that place.

He settled for an imperceptible shake of his head.

Would she pick up on it? Would it discourage her from picking a fight?

They were outnumbered. Now was the time to regroup, to come up with a plan.

The banditos escorted them back to the wagon where Father Emmanuel sat, bound and gagged.

Soon, they were all loaded into the cart, trussed up in the same fashion.

The ride back to town was a silent one, but Matthew prayed and planned, then prayed and planned some more.

Would they escape Jericho this time?

Chapter Twenty-Two

"You can't be serious!" John slammed his fist down on the desk in front of him. He couldn't believe that an army colonel would refuse to help him rescue American citizens.

Colonel Herman squared himself, his deadpan stare drilling into John.

"Sheriff Durbin," he began, "I understand your concern for your friends. However, the United States Army can't just march into Mexico with demands that they be released."

"I know that," John admitted, "but I'm not asking for you to send in troops. I'm just looking for a couple of good men to go with me in the off-chance that things get a little rough. You know, just to even the numbers a little."

Colonel Herman shook his head. "One man or one hundred – it doesn't make a difference," the Colonel explained. He drummed his fingers on the desk, his expression suggesting that the debated on whether to continue or not. "Listen, the truth is that I really can't afford to send anyone right now."

"Why not?" Frustrated, John raised his hands in question. "They're American citizens who were taken off their own soil. We have a right to do what we can to protect our own!"

"I agree." Colonel Herman clasped his hands together and leaned over the desk. "All right, here's the problem. Now mind you, what I'm about to say doesn't leave this room, because you don't have the proper security clearance. I really shouldn't be telling you this at all, but I understand what it's like to lose good people to bad reasons.

"You have my solemn word that whatever you have to say lives and dies right here," John promised, his eyes intent as he leaned closer to the desk.

"Well, it's like this," the Colonel began. "I recently received an anonymous letter from someone claiming to be one of Pancho Villa's ex-officers. The letter stated that an attack on Nogales – this very fort – was planned for the twenty-fifth of August."

"That was two days ago." John sat back, crossing his arms. "Nothing's happened yet. It could be that someone was just having a bit of fun with you – not that there's much humor in the matter."

"I'm not so sure about that." Colonel Herman busied himself with papers that littered the desk. "Some of our men like to sneak over to a little saloon right across the way. The locals call it Jericho. Something like that. I used to look the other way – figuring that it would make them a little less rowdy in ranks. But then I started getting reports a couple of weeks back about a group of Mexican men talking to some German soldiers and gathering supplies. Ammunition, weapons, the sort."

John let out a low whistle.

"Exactly," Colonel Herman responded. "An American soldier walking into Mexico right now might just set off a battle. Add to the fact that I've had to

220

medically discharge a few men, and you can see I really don't have anyone to spare."

Colonel Herman stood, indicating their meeting was over, just as a soldier walked in to report to him.

"I'm sorry, Sheriff Durbin. I really do hope you find your friends."

Realizing that he was being dismissed, John stood as well. He placed his dusty hat back on his head and reached out a hand.

"I understand. You've got to do what you've got to do," he said, flattening his curly mop of hair with his hat. He swatted away the dust particles floating in front of his face. "But realize that I've got to do what I've got to do, too."

Then, John turned around and marched out of the colonel's office.

Looked like he was on his own.

Looked like she was on her own again.

Catalina squinted through swollen eyes, then she slammed them shut. Seriously? Back in here again? So it hadn't been a nightmare. This place was the real deal.

"That was a really stupid thing to do."

Catalina could barely make out the figure in the dark room she occupied, but she recognized the voice. The stench... Old alcohol and sweat mixed with cheap perfume.

Her words came out as muffled grunts and she nearly choked on her own tongue.

"Wait a minute." Mercedes sighed and stepped into the dim morning light that shone through a single dirt-caked window. She untied Catalina's gag and pulled an extra cloth from her mouth. "Ay, Catalina. They double gagged you... stupid girl." She shook her head.

Catalina finally found her voice. "I would appreciate it if you would stop calling me stupid," she croaked. "I only did what I had to so I could escape."

"Ay, but you didn't escape. Did you?" Mercedes placed one hand on her hip, the other one dismissing Catalina's bravado. "No. You had to land yourself in the worst room in the house!"

Catalina silently chided herself that the greatest error she committed was getting Matthew and her wayward *prima* involved. Well, it was taking a great deal of prayer for Catalina to remind herself that she was Christian and shouldn't wish ill on anyone – not even the likes of Amorina. Matthew, on the other hand, was an entirely different story altogether. He had already been through so much, and all of it tied back to her.

No, you can't think like that.

Catalina refused to allow misplaced guilt to overcome her again. Wasn't there some kind of saying about God helping those who helped themselves? Well, feeling sorry for herself certainly wasn't going to help any.

What she needed was another escape plan and... Matthew.

Catalina surveyed her surroundings, but she could make out very little in the dark room. A squeaky wooden chair, the one she was bound to, appeared to be the sole furnishing.

Bound with ropes so tight it was little wonder she hadn't lost circulation to her hands.

"It doesn't seem that bad." She tried to infuse a little humor into the situation. "Just needs a bit of sprucing up. I'm pretty handy with a scrub brush."

Mercedes placed both hands on her hips this time. "Are you seriously making jokes at a time like this?" She huffed.

Catalina sighed. "I was just trying to get my mind off these ropes. They're cutting into my wrists." She struggled a little against the tension, but the burning pain that seared through her arms forced her to stop. "You wouldn't be able to undo them for me. Would you?"

"Not on your life or mine," Mercedes wagged a finger at her. "And it would probably be mine. No, *amiga.* I just slipped in here to see how you were holding up." She paused, then added an afterthought. "How about a drink of water?"

Catalina forced a smile and accepted the meager offer. "Yes, please. That would be nice."

Mercedes eased the door open and peered out. She ducked out of the room, and returned just as quick with a bucket of water. She drew up the ladle and offered it to Catalina. "Slow down or you will make yourself sick," Mercedes admonished. "Not that it matters anyway. You'll probably end up like Eloisa. Then again, I bet we all will."

Catalina jerked her head up. What had happened to Eloisa? "What are you talking about?" she asked. "It was only yesterday that she told us she was getting married."

"Yes, and it was only last night that she was murdered," Mercedes informed her. "The man who came to get her didn't really want a wife. He was just an animal and wanted to take out his hatred against someone. Of course, there's only so much you can do to one of Belmonte's women – that is, unless you purchase her. So the man did." Mercedes hung her head with a heavy sigh. "They found her body this morning."

Catalina stared at Mercedes. It was difficult to wrap her mind around the idea that anyone could do something so hideous to another person.

"Why?" she asked, still trying to sort through the confounding information. "And how do you even know?"

"I already told you why." Mercedes placed the ladle back in the bucket and stood. "And I know because I heard some of the men debating if they should bury her and El Perro together, or just burn the bodies."

Catalina shuddered at the thought of such an improper burial. Wait a minute! El Perro? Dread pitted in her belly. Was she responsible for another man's death? "What happened to El Perro?"

Mercedes shrugged. "He let you escape."

Catalina sat upright, but dizziness made the room whirl. She held her head until the spell passed. "What? Wait a minute." She shook her head. Unbelievable! Fear morphed into anger. "Are you telling me that Belmonte killed him just because I got away? That's absolutely insane! He didn't know what I had planned and—"

"And had he known," a voice from the doorway spoke with lethal precision, "then I would've still killed him for arranging to meet with you in private."

Belmonte slid into the room like a serpent.

Shivers skittered down Catalina's spine. She sat up a little straighter, and the tight bonds contracted around her wrists. Her skin was raw from abuse, and she could feel the blood begin to ooze down the palm of her hands.

She flashed a cautious glanced over to Mercedes, but Belmonte followed her gaze.

"Tsk, tsk." Belmonte stared at Mercedes, drawing it out in an intentional display of his power, his nostrils flaring. One hand shot out, sudden as a serpent's strike, and he wrapped a handful of the woman's hair around his hand. "What are you doing here, Mercedes? I don't recall giving you permission to talk to this *perra*."

"It's my fault." Catalina tried to cover for Mercedes.

"It's your fault that Mercedes came in here on her own accord?" Belmonte dismissed her misplaced bravado.

"No, Jefe. It was my fault," Mercedes tried to bow her head with reverence, but he held her hair even tighter. "I know that she is important to your business, and saw that the men weren't caring for her. So I came in only to make sure that she did not die of thirst." She held up the ladle, liquid slurping over the sides. "See? I only brought water."

Her comrade cowered before the man who held both their lives in his hand with the expertise of someone who had worked for the man a long time.

Belmonte studied one woman and then the other. With an abrupt release, he excused Mercedes from the room. "Next time, you will ask for my permission."

Silently conceding to his wishes, Mercedes bowed as she backed out of the room, leaving Catalina alone to face the wrath of a man who had lost two commodities in one night.

"You think you are something so special," Belmonte spat out the accusation as if it held a bitter taste. He paced back and forth in front of Catalina, his head bowed as though in deep thought.

Some of his men entered the room with a table and set it before her.

Finally, he spoke, "You come in here and try to turn my girls against me with your talk of God. Then you take advantage of my men and try to escape. After all I have done for you? I have ensured that no man has touched you. I have allowed you to walk about the grounds as you please, and have kept you fed and clothed. And this is how you repay me?"

Belmonte shook his head as though admonishing a small child.

"You should be punished," he continued, as a couple of men filed in with chairs. "In fact, any other woman would have been whipped and given to one of my men for his liking."

Catalina glared at the man with utter contempt, biting the words lingering on the tip of her tongue.

Belmonte had proven that he truly was an evil man by having one of his own saloon hands killed. For the simple mistake of being outwitted.

"But I know how to take care of you, love." He continued speaking as several working girls – La Fea and two new faces – entered, their arms filled with dishes of food. They smoothed out a white table cloth and set the table as though preparing for a banquet.

Delicious smells wafted through the air from the colorful clay pots filled with traditional Mexican dishes.

Catalina instinctively sniffed the air – a long, slow intake of breath that forced her stomach to rumble with anticipation. After nearly a day without food, she was weak and could barely think. As her brain began to fog over from the enticing aromas, she tried to focus on Belmonte's words.

What had he said about *her* benefactor?

He motioned for two men to move her to a chair. Then he sat down across from her. "I'm not too sure he would appreciate your new look, though."

La Fea served his food and returned to a corner of the room, her gaze focused on the floor in front of her.

With a mouthful of food, Belmonte said, "No. Definitely not. We will have to fix that."

Catalina sniffed and held her head a little higher. She had to have faith that freedom was soon at hand. Until then, she wasn't going to allow any man to subject her to indecencies that betrayed her morals.

"I am a child of God." She spoke calmly. "And I'm not going to get dolled up for a man just so I can end up like Eloisa."

Belmonte stopped chewing. His eyes turned into two little slits in his head and he swallowed.

"There's a small part of me that admires your courage. It's the same wild spirit I find in a prized stag." A smug look danced across Belmonte's face. "However, there is an even greater part of me that would enjoy watching you whipped and broken like a good mare."

Before Catalina could respond, Belmonte stood and leaned over the table.

She pushed as far back in the chair as she could, but that only caused Belmonte to smile at her fear.

"Now shut up and eat."

He snapped his fingers behind him and La Fea rushed to Catalina's side to spoon some *frijoles* into a tortilla. Catalina accepted the taco with a small smile. "Thank you."

"That's more like it," Belmonte responded without looking at her, apparently unaware that Catalina had been speaking to the other woman. "You should be thanking me for seeing to your kind treatment when you could have been thrown to the men like that other girl.

Realizing she was in a delicate position, Catalina chose to remain silent. Instead, she continued taking small bites of food and downed the delicious brew, quenching her thirst. It tasted of honeyed rice milk.

And something else.

Catalina looked up at the woman so kindly serving her, but the woman didn't meet her gaze, only hung her head.

Something was wrong.

Her feet tingled…

Trying to make sense of the numbness that had started to spread through her body, Catalina stared at Belmonte.

Sitting back with his arms crossed in front of his chest, he raised an interested brow.

"Are you feeling okay, *nena*?" His voice betrayed his mocking look of concern. "No? Well, that is no surprise. You see, I have to make you presentable to *el güero* who has purchased you. However, your little attempts at running away make me think that you are not so trustworthy. You know?"

Belmonte paused as though expecting Catalina to refute his accusations.

But she couldn't force her lips to move. Drool slithered down her chin.

He nodded as if she had responded.

"Yes, I think it is safe to say that you won't be causing any more trouble. See, we need to bathe you, fix your hair, put on the pretty dress… Oh, so much work! And I can't have you trying to run away again, or fighting to look presentable like La Fea used to." Belmonte shot a nasty look at the woman standing against the wall, still as a statue. "But no one will pay *ni un peso* – not one little cent – for La Fea. But you… Oh, for you… They will keep me in business for the rest of the year! So, I think to myself 'Belmonte, what you gonna' do with this one? She is so stubborn. She makes it too difficult always.' But I have to do something, because it'll be a few hours before I can get rid of you. So that's when I come up with this little idea for the drink."

The blood drained from Catalina's face, and nausea swelled.

"What did you give me?" she muttered between the drool and double vision of Belmonte.

He took another bite of food and chewed, calm and cool, as if debating on whether or not she deserved an answer.

He shrugged. "Morphine."

It made no difference. The word hardly registered as Catalina drifted off.

Matthew landed on the cold floor with a solid thud. Double knots laced his hands and feet, so he could do nothing to break the fall. His head bounced off the concrete, pain arcing through his whole body.

"Don't even think of trying to escape," his assailant said. "There'll be a guard right outside. Then *El Jefe* will decide what to do with you – right after he finishes with that little *sucia* of yours."

Matthew ground his teeth at the indication that he and Catalina had been immoral.

I'm going to need some serious help here, Lord. First, with my temper, and second, to get us out of this mess!

"Who knows?" The man continued to antagonize him. "Maybe I do a good job and Belmonte will let me have a piece of her, too."

Matthew glared, keeping his expression deadpan, giving away nothing, as emotionless as calm seas after a torrential storm – any damage undetectable to the naked eye.

Realizing that he wouldn't get a rise out of Matthew, the man grunted and left the room. The sound of the heavy door slamming behind him echoed throughout the room, and Matthew let out a slow exhale.

Finally!

Matthew studied the knots that laced his hands and feet. He had taken great measures to set himself up for an escape.

As a teen, he had once seen a show featuring an illusionist named Harry Houdini. After the show, he went up to the man and boldly asked what his secret was. The man had leaned over and whispered that there wasn't any secret, but only a few illusionary tricks that deceived the eye. Over the years, he tried practicing escape attempts with another deputy. Nothing ever seemed to work, though.

Lord, please let it work this time.

When the *banditos* tied him up, he had taken in as much air as possible and held it as they wrapped the rope around him. Then he had tightened up every muscle in his body. Now alone, he relaxed and surveyed the room. A bed, table with two chairs and thick oak wardrobe. Nothing appeared very useful.

Was this Catalina's room? Did she have to do things against her will – against God's will – just to survive? What actually happened to her while she was here?

Unanswered questions assaulted his mind, and his body became taut against the rope again, biting into his wrists.

Why hadn't he asked her what her experience had been like? The very idea that she may have been abused had failed to cross his mind earlier. He had just been so grateful to see her alive and well – amazingly delivered right to him as though decreed by Divine Providence.

Trust in the Lord with all thine heart, and lean not upon thine own understanding.

Matthew acknowledged the small voice that steeled his resolve. He would have noticed a change in Catalina had anything happened to her.

No.

He was confident that God had protected Catalina after she had been sold to this house of sin and shame, and he was equally sure that this had all happened for a very good reason. Why, he wasn't too sure of yet.

But, that wasn't the main concern at the moment. Time to concentrate on finding a way to escape.

Allowing himself to completely relax again, his muscles loosened. He let out every bit of air. The ropes gave just a little.

Matthew stared at the floor to the side of him – focusing on a small square of wood that had splintered from years of use, until it blurred, and the double vision turned the splinter into two pieces. The entire time, Matthew moved the lower muscles in his arm, sweat beading on his face and dripping on the floor. The rope around his midsection had tightened while the part around his arms had loosened some, and he was drenched by the time he freed one hand from the knotted mess.

Matthew gritted out a smile, satisfied with his progress. It was only a matter of time before he would work his way out of these bonds.

And back to Catalina.

But would he be too late?

Chapter Twenty-Three

"Hey there, señorita."

Mercedes's back shot up straight as a rod. She twisted around from her kneeling position and looked up at the *güero* who spoke to her through the courtyard's closed gates.

He raised his hat in a salutation.

Her mouth dropped open. She had been at Jericho long enough to have seen just about every kind of man imaginable, including many Americans, but she had never met anyone with such red hair!

Surprised by the sudden rush of attraction, Mercedes stood. Her skirt full of medicinal plants fell back to the earth and she brushed the dirt off her apron. She wiped the back of one hand across her eyes. Had the handsome stranger heard her pitiful crying? Anger filled her. Although she wasn't sure if it was because she had been caught unaware, or if it was because she had allowed herself to get to close to that American girl.

"Who are you? What do you want?" she asked, her accent thick with emotion. She stood in the middle of her little garden, a hand now placed on each round hip. "I don't know what you're looking for, but I'm not working right now."

John's eyes narrowed at both the woman's admission and assumption. He had seen more than his fair share of working ladies back in Abilene. However, none of them were as beautiful as the Mexican rose who stood in defiance before him right now. Her graceful chin in the air, hands on shapely hips, with plants littering the ground beside her petite feet.

John frowned.

Not that he would have ever had the inclination to pay for such services, no matter how beautiful the woman. As the sheriff of a bustling town on the verge of becoming a city, he had been too busy chasing down criminals to find enough time to pursue a relationship.

Besides, God would send the right one when the appropriate time came.

I just hope it happens before I lose any more hair.

John slapped his hat back on his thinning head, stamping out any romantic thoughts with it. "Ma'am, don't you think it's a might presumptuous to just assume I'm even interested in you like that?"

The woman opened her mouth, but nothing came out. She slid some hair back from her face, and smiled, beautiful, and somewhat rusty.

He waved away any possible explanation. "I'm sorry to be so blunt, ma'am, especially regarding such a delicate topic, but I'm here on important business. You see, a couple of my friends have disappeared, and I have it on good authority that they might be right here in this very saloon. Now you wouldn't know anything about that, would you?"

The woman squirmed, looking anxious and uncomfortable. She eyed him with suspicion. "Maybe I do," she responded. "But why should I tell you anything? I don't know who you are. Maybe you're not really their friend... maybe you're looking to kill someone."

John dug into his pocket, held out his badge.

She took a cautious step closer and peered through the iron rods.

"Oh, all right." The woman must have decided that he was one of the good guys after all. "We've had several new shipments in the last few weeks. Which ones are yours? Are they adults or children?"

John balked.

Shipments? Children?

His jaw dropped at the idea of people being sold into slavery as easily as they sold cattle back home in the meat market. What could anyone possibly want with a small child?

He rubbed his face with his hands, trying to wipe out the contrived images of mistreated children.

"They're American," he finally said. "A deputy by the name of Matthew and a little bitty gal, Catalina."

Mercedes gasped at the mention of her friend's name.

"Yes. Yes, I know her." Her gaze darted around the courtyard before hustling over to the iron gates. She squeezed her face through the rails, gripping until her knuckles turned white. "I don't know the man, but I know Catalina. She is always causing trouble, that one. She has a good heart, though. Oh, I can't bear to think what they'll do to her."

The woman wiped away a single tear, and his heart ached for her and everyone behind the prison bars. He didn't know what her story was, but no one should be forced to live like a slave.

He wrapped his hands around hers, surprised at the strength and the passion that sizzled through them.

"All right, here's what we're going to do." John quickly unfolded a plan to help rescue Catalina. With any luck, they would find Matthew shortly thereafter.

Mercedes listened in awe as the stranger agreed to come back for her once he had settled Catalina back in the United States.

Breathless, she agreed to his plan and scurried back to her small garden.

Catalina stirred at the tinkling sound. Was it time for afternoon tea with her mother? Her lips curved. Would Mother serve scones this afternoon or biscuits with the blackberry jam she loved so much?

Her eyelids fluttered open, revealing the cold, sterile room.

The smile faded. This was not home.

Something clinked again. Her head whipped to the sound.

"You!" Catalina sat up straight, the tight ropes again cutting into her wrists. She stared at the scarred face smiling at her from the opposite end of the table, newly set as if to host an afternoon tea.

A mixture of fear and disgust flowed through her veins as the man added cream and sugar to his cup. What game was he playing?

"Why, darling, I didn't think you'd remember me." The man lifted the saucer that supported his teacup and brought the hot drink to his lips, completely draining it as would a man thirsting for water.

It only served as proof to Catalina that his refined appearance was nothing more than a small part of an elaborate lie.

He placed his empty cup back on the table. "It's been a few weeks since we've seen each other. So I had some doubt that you would recall our last meeting. I guess I'm more memorable than I thought."

His Southern drawl grated against her nerves.

"Sir, I would dare to say that's putting it mildly," she seethed. "I knew there was something strange and evil about you, even from the moment I saw you on that ferry back in Mississippi. I suspected then that you were following me. However, I didn't – and still don't – understand why you've made me your target. What have I ever done to you?"

The man's countenance suddenly turned from viciously playful to disturbingly frightful.

"What have you ever done to me?" The question came out as a growl. The man flashed a crooked grin at her and stood. He was before her in an instant – his face lowered mere inches from hers. His hot breath fell on her face, the rancid smell of it assaulting her senses as he barked at her. "What have you done to me? Interesting how I easily remember you, but you don't recall me in the least. I remember when you were but a girl, though. I can see now that you haven't changed a bit. You were a wretched prima donna then and still are."

Catalina shook her head, confused. "I'm sorry, but I—I don't understand." She stammered as the man straightened. She looked up at the man and studied his features. But other than the ferry, she drew a blank. "Sir, I really don't know how I could have offended you."

"Ah, well. I suppose it has been a number of years since we've last seen each other." The man gave a careless shrug before awarding her with a mock bow. "Allow me to reintroduce myself… Christopher Monroe, at your service."

Catalina's heart fluttered, and her chest constricted as if the very air she breathed was being squeezed out of her lungs. White spots formed in her vision and she felt as though the earth beneath her would instantaneously give way. Or maybe that's what she wished to happen?

Catalina strained to focus on the man's expression, finally registering some of the familiar features from his brother's face.

"You do look a little bit like Ben."

Christopher's face darkened.

"You are never… NEVER… to say his name again. You hear me?"

A string of expletives spewed from his mouth as he grabbed the sides of her chair and shook her.

Tears welled up in her eyes. "I'm so—sorry," she stammered. She sucked in air.

"Stop it! Just stop it," he yelled at her before releasing the chair. He stood back up and wiped the back of his hand across his own face – sniffing back any emotion before it could escape. He turned back to where he had been sitting and picked up the knife from beside his plate. Turning to Catalina, he lifted the blade with a smile.

"You," he said in a strange sing-song fashion. He waved the knife around as he waltzed back towards her. "You are so right, my precious little doll. Did you know that? Did you know that I always thought of you as some pretty little doll? A brat to be certain, but there was never any doubting your beauty, my dear. Still, you are so very right because you will indeed be sorry by the time I get through with you."

Tremors ran down Catalina's spine. "What are you going to do?"

"Shhh," Christopher silenced her as he brandished the blade in front of her face. "I'm just going to have what my brother couldn't have," he whispered. Then he ran the flat side of the knife softly down her cheek.

"Then I'm going to make it so you're not so pretty anymore."

Hot tears fell down Catalina's face. Why was this happening?

Please, God. Please save me.

She looked heavenward.

Was Matthew safe or had they already killed him? Fearing for his life and hers, she squeezed her eyes shut.

Lord, save us.

Chapter Twenty-Four

Matthew yanked off the remaining rope that wove around his ankles. He stood, his legs a little shaky, and stretched out his taut muscles.

He had originally questioned whether or not he could really get out of his bonds. He looked down now at the tangled mass, evidence that his escape would have rivaled even that of the great Houdini.

Thank You, Lord!

He swiped the sweat off his face. What should he do next?

The bedroom door squeaked. Then, someone pushed it open.

He grabbed for the closest thing to him and held it up in defense.

"What are you going to do with that?" A woman asked, sarcasm lacing her tone as she eased the door closed. She pointed to the straw broom in Matthew's hands. "Hit me over the head with it? I doubt that flimsy thing would do much damage. It barely sweeps the room."

Matthew slowly lowered the broom.

"I didn't have much time to think," he replied. "Who are you anyway?"

"Mercedes, a friend of Catalina's. Someone came to the gate looking for you. Sheriff John Durbin. He

240

wants to help get you both out." The woman twisted her head around to check the door.

"John! So that old coot's still around? I wondered what happened to him." Matthew said. "So what exactly did you have in mind?"

"The best thing to do is to get out of here. Don't you think?" Mercedes asked.

"Well, of course I do." Matthew responded. "I just don't think it would be a successful escape if I have to go up against a bunch of armed men without my gun."

"Oh, that." Mercedes shrugged and pulled out a small bag of what looked like a bunch of dried plants. "I don't think you'll have to do too much fighting against anyone. Most of them finished the noon meal and are busy, um, relieving themselves."

She held the bag out and waited for Matthew to accept it.

"What is it?" he asked as he studied the bag.

"An old Nahutl friend." Mercedes crossed her arms in front of her chest and smiled, as if proud of herself.

Matthew nodded his head in understanding.

"*Epazote*," he said, remembering his grandmother using it as a cure-all for bellyaches. Too much of it could be toxic, though. He handed the bag back. "Glad to know you're on our side. Please, lead the way."

"I guess I could be something of a gentleman, and make you just a smidge more comfortable." Christopher Monroe leaned closer still to Catalina. He sawed through the ropes that bound her to the arms of the chair. "In fact, I think we'd both benefit. Don't you agree?"

Catalina chose not to answer. Instead, she scanned the room for anything that would assist her to defend herself.

Chair. Table. Dishes. A single fork. Not much to work with.

If I aim just so, then I could do a fair deal of damage with it.

"What do you think, darling?" Christopher whispered in her ear just as the ropes behind her back snapped. "The floor would do just fine, wouldn't it?"

Catalina pulled her knees close to her chest and gave a good, swift kick. The sudden movement caught Christopher square in the chest and he flew backward with a resounding thud.

"Maybe for you, but not for me!" she yelled.

She jumped up and shook off the remaining ropes that wound around her legs and feet. She dove for the fork on the table just as Christopher stood back up.

"Nuh-uh. I don't think so, darling." Christopher lunged forward, bringing the knife down in a slashing motion.

Catalina screamed and hopped back. She grabbed hold of the chair, using it as a barrier between her and the murderous madman.

But, he seized the chair and yanked it out from her. He hurled it across the room, and it careened against the far side of the wall, cracking and obliterating into a handful of sticks.

She made a run for the table, but Christopher reached out and grasped a handful of her hair.

Catalina fell back with a cry.

"Oooh, I do love me a woman with some fight!" Christopher's throaty voice blew hot breath her way. Turning her to face him, he presented her with a sickening smile before pushing forward to plant a hard kiss on her lips. His revolting breath made her gag.

He laughed and leaned in again.

POP! POP! POP!

Several guns fired off shots outside.

Christopher stepped back, his face a mixture of surprise and alarm. Yelling from the courtyard floated up to the saloon's window.

Firmly gripping Catalina's arm, Christopher dragged her towards the small square window. He pushed it forward and surveyed the ground below.

Catalina leaned around him and peeked at the scene. Several men ran through the streets, rifles in their hands. More quickly followed behind them. La Fea lugged a basket of clothes on one hip, seemingly unfazed by the commotion.

"Hey, you." Her companion called down, annoyance tainting his tone. "What's going on down there?"

La Fea gave him an unintelligible stare.

Good for her!

He repeated himself in Spanish, but she only shrugged.

"Stupid Mexican," he spat before slamming the window shut.

"Maybe you should ask Belmonte," Catalina suggested. If she could get rid of him, her chances at escape magnified. Especially with all the commotion downstairs. They might forget about her for a while.

"That's exactly what I intend to do."

Still holding onto her arm with a vice-like grip, he tugged her towards the door when it suddenly flew open.

Mercedes stood in the doorway, her hands clutched to her chest. "Please, *señor*. We must leave now! The Americans are attacking!"

"What?" Christopher rushed out into the hall. As soon as he did, Mercedes grabbed Catalina's other arm and yanked her back towards the room.

The moment the connection broke, Matthew flew through the air and tackled the very surprised Christopher. Both men tumbled down the long set of stairs leading into Jericho's main saloon, tangling as they bumped their way to the first floor.

"Be careful, Matthew! He's armed," Catalina yelled, scurrying after him with Mercedes hot on her heels.

"No, you mustn't!" Mercedes urged her to leave. "We have to get you to the horses."

"But I can't leave him," Catalina cried.

The men wrestled on the empty saloon floor.

"*Si te toca, te toca*," Mercedes insisted and gave her a final shove towards the front door. "He'll take care of himself, or God will!"

She stumbled outside, the brilliant sunlight blinding her.

"Come on, gal!" A familiar voice urged her to look up.

Sheriff Durbin waved her forward, the other hand gripping reins for two horses.

"John!" Catalina rushed towards him.

He held out one arm and she slammed into his side. "It's good to see you, gal."

"You, too! I was afraid I'd never see the outside of these prison walls."

"Hey, now. That's my woman you're hugging."

"Matthew!" Catalina turned, relief making her knees weak. She reached out with a bold hand to frame his cheek. She cringed at the sight of a swollen eye. "I thought for sure you'd be a goner."

"Not quite," Matthew reassured her, covering her hand with his. "Although, I don't suggest we stick around here too long. No telling when that lunatic is liable to wake up." He took the reins from John's outstretched hand.

"Exactly why we need to move out," John mounted and extended a hand to Mercedes. "You coming?"

Catalina's gaze swapped between her friends. Would Mercedes choose freedom? "Please, Mercedes? Hurry!"

Mercedes looked up at John. Then back at the saloon. She gave them a tight smile. "Maybe next time," she said.

John looked at her hard. A lump crawled down his whiskered throat. Then, he tipped the brim of his hat before riding off.

Matthew's hands curled around her waist and hoisted her up onto the horse. Then he swung up behind her, adjusting his fingers around the reins.

Catalina glanced down at Mercedes, a strange mixture of relief and sadness washing over her. "Thank you for helping us," she said. "I'll never forget you."

Mercedes nodded, tears filling her red-rimmed eyes.

"Yah!" Matthew stuck his heels into the side of the horse and they took off into the vast desert.

Epilogue

Charlotte, North Carolina – Four Months Later

Catalina ran her fingers over the wedding dress, the soft satin detailed with small, white lace roses around the neckline. Each held a pretty pink pearl in the center.

"Oh, Mama. Those pearls came from the first piece of jewelry Papa ever gave you." Catalina rushed over to her mother and gave her a hug. "You really shouldn't have."

Teresa Santé beamed at her daughter.

"Of course, I should have!" she exclaimed. "It's not every day that my only daughter gets married."

The two hugged again, at least the hundredth since she'd arrived back home.

"You're lucky to marry that one off at all!"

Catalina turned as her older brother, Gabe, sauntered into her room.

"And you, sir, are supposed to knock." She reached up and gave his nose a little pinch. It was impossible to truly be upset with his teasing, though. He had requested special permission to take leave from his studies just to attend her wedding. She gave him a hug. "Oh, Gabe. I'm so glad you're here."

"Me, too." Gabe returned the embrace, then released her. "I just wish I could have gotten here a few days earlier. It would have been nice to become acquainted with this Matthew fellow you plan on marrying."

Catalina's hands rushed to her cheeks as she tried to cover her embarrassment.

"Oh, no! I completely forgot to tell you that I invited him for tea today, Mama."

"You did?" Her mother's face drooped. "Oh, Cat. I don't know if we have any biscuits or cookies left, and I question if I can whip up either before he gets here. Why didn't you say something? You know I'm just starting to get the hang of this whole cooking thing!"

Her mother fanned away oncoming tears.

"Don't worry, Mama. I'll take care of everything." Catalina tried to soothe her mother while Gabe took the hysterics as a good sign to leave. "You just worry about finishing up the dress, and putting it away. I'll go down to prepare the tea." After all, she probably had more experience than her mother now. Something good had come from Jericho.

Catalina gave her mother's arm a pat before leaving the room. She had been having a difficult time adjusting to life without servants. However, both the unfaithful cook and maid had to be put out when the family learned that they had betrayed Catalina's whereabouts to the Monroe family.

All for a few worthless greenbacks.

Catalina shook her head as she headed down the stairs. She'd go straightaway to the kitchen and see what afternoon delight she could create. How hard could it be? Baking a few biscuits couldn't be that much different from making tortillas, right? She rolled up her shirt sleeves as she landed on the bottom step, her attention snagged by Matthew's deep voice from the parlor.

She poked her head through the door. "Well, it seems like you two have already become acquainted."

Catalina nodded at her brother and moved over to stand beside Matthew, smiling up into his ocean blue eyes. She didn't know how it was possible, but he managed to look more handsome each time she saw him.

"Hello, love." Matthew smiled back, and wrapped her arm into the crook of his own.

"Eh hem." Gabe cleared his throat. "Mr. Martin was just about to deliver some news, I believe."

Matthew straightened his back, but didn't let go of her arm.

"That's right," he said, reaching into his pocket. "I just got a letter from John."

Catalina brightened. "Really? What did he write?" She released his arm so that he could open the letter.

"Well, first he apologized for not being able to attend the wedding." Matthew unfolded the letter and read it out loud.

He informed them of how Christopher Monroe had tried crossing into the United States during the border battle, only to be mistaken as a Mexican and shot on sight.

Gabe pounded a fist into his hand. "Serves the traitor right!"

"Gabe!" Catalina admonished. She was relieved not to worry about another Monroe brother coming after her, but she certainly didn't delight in anyone's death.

"Well, no bad tree bears good fruit." Her brother stood firm in his belief.

Catalina speared a questioning glance at Matthew. Did he feel the same?

"He's right," Matthew agreed. "The letter even states that the *banditos* were looking for him because he never did pay up all the money he owed them for taking you. If the army hadn't gotten him, then the Jericho gang would have. And that would have been a far worth death to suffer."

"Exactly!" Gabe agreed. "Mind if I relay some of this information to my father?"

Matthew handed over the letter and Gabe bolted from the room.

"And what do you think about all this?" Matthew's eyes searched Catalina's face.

"I think you may be right. God's word teaches that bad associations spoil useful habits. The loss of both the Monroe boys serve as proof that the words were true."

She hesitated, unanswered questions still churning through her brain. But what about the women and children who had been left behind at Jericho? Many of them did bad, but it was against their will. If they didn't, then they would be beaten or even killed. The only possible option was to try to escape, but that could very well have deadly results, too. Fight or die trying. That seemed to be Mexico's law of the land.

Catalina shook her head. She wasn't sure what John's exact plans were, whether he would attempt another rescue of Mercedes, but she prayed that God would watch him every step of the way.

"A penny for your thoughts," Matthew said.

"They're worth much more than that," she responded with a playful hand on his arm. But then she grew serious again. "I was just thinking about John's letter. I hope everything goes well."

Matthew nodded in agreement.

"I hope as well." He drew her closer to his side. "He's a good man, smart and wise. He'll be careful. But, I have a hunch that all the lawlessness in Jericho isn't the only thing calling him back."

Catalina smiled, recalling their ride back to the States. John had shown a real range of emotions – from silence to anger and finally concern – when Mercedes had turned down his offer to leave with them. Then an interrogation had ensued as John tried to pump Catalina for as much information as possible. He wanted to know everything she did about Mercedes, the men who guarded the saloon and even Jericho's layout. The more she talked, the clearer it became that John was planning some sort of rescue.

"I think you're right," Catalina finally said. "The more I think about it, the surer I am that John might be a bit smitten with Mercedes."

Matthew threw back his head, his throaty laughter filling the air. "You think? Maybe you got that impression when he mentioned riding in to rescue the girl 'like a knight in shining armor?'"

His expression grew serious as he wrapped his arms around her. "I'd venture to say he's more than smitten if he feels for her even an inkling of what I feel for you."

Heat rushed to her cheeks. She bit her bottom lip, her stomach giddy with anticipation.

Matthew lowered his head to hers, inch by delicious inch, until his lips landed on her, sending a shiver down her spine. He lingered only a moment longer before gently releasing her.

Catalina laid her head on his chest and melted into him. The feel of his strong arms offered a future of love and protection.

Her rebel heart could finally rest.

A Letter to Readers:

Again, thank you so much for picking up a copy of *A Rebel in Jericho*. Everything you've read in this book is fictional. However, there are a couple of passages that are based on true historical facts. I wanted to share the real accounts behind those scenes for anyone interested in such information.

On page nineteen, I refer to a "crazy storm" that washed away Robert Harrington's business. Well, there was no Robert Harrington in real life (not as far as I know, leastways). However, there really was a tremendous storm that took place in 1916. Western North Carolina was devastated with more death and destruction than the State had ever seen before from a natural disaster. In fact, one spot in Grandfather Mountain registered 22 inches of rain in less than a single day! The course of the Swannanoa River was changed, and residents found themselves with no way out. Homes and businesses were destroyed, countless lives lost and the state would never be the same again.

However, North Carolina wasn't the only place seeing disaster. In a time of much change and progress, factories were on the rise – especially with the men off to war. One of these factories (referred to on page six) was The Triangle Shirtwaist Factory in Manhattan. March 25, 1911 marks the day of one of the deadliest industrial disasters ever recorded in U.S. history, when this factory sealed exit doors to keep workers in. When an accidental fire broke out, 146 individuals (namely Italian and Jewish immigrant woman) were killed.

Also, the setup for the final scenes were based off a real customs incident during a border crossing. When a Mexican man failed to stop at customs and declare what he was leaving the country with, a U.S. soldier shot at him. Mexican residents thought the army was attacking and took up arms to defend themselves. The U.S. soldiers fired in return, under the mistaken belief that the Mexicans and Germans had sided together in an attack.

All these historical facts can be found in any number of places. An internet search, library books and newspaper articles are all available should you be interested in further research. Personally, I thoroughly enjoyed reading about these occurrences. It helped me gain a greater appreciation for the struggles on individuals living in the early 1900's.

Lastly, I welcome you to connect with me if you enjoyed reading this story. Oftentimes, I look for people who would like to critique or review my books in exchange for advance reader copies. If you believe you would be interested in participating (or simply want to know when the next book is coming out), then please visit me at:

writemimimilan@gmail.com
www.mimimilan.com
www.facebook.com/AuthorMimiMilan
www.twitter.com/thewritingMimi

For those of you who prefer snail mail, please write me at:

Mimi Milan
PO Box 19795
Charlotte, NC 28219-0795

Coming Soon

The Jericho Resistance | Book Two

Twice Redeemed